THE GHOST OF BRANSCOMBE PLATS

THE GHOST OF BRANSCOMBE PLATS
Copyright © Philippa Moseley 2003

ISBN 1-84426-236-7

First published 2003 by
UPFRONT PUBLISHING LTD
Leicestershire

Printed by Lightning Source

The Ghost of Branscombe Plats

PHILIPPA MOSELEY

UPFRONT PUBLISHING
LEICESTERSHIRE

To my husband and for Helena

CHAPTER 1

During a heat wave in July, Triffy Garland finally made up her mind to run away from the children's home in Sidmouth where she'd lived for the two years since her mother's death.

She packed a bottle of water, a torch, a penknife, a pair of scissors, a tee shirt, underwear, a cardigan, a toothbrush and flannel and her precious home-made catapult, into a rucksack. Creeping downstairs to the deserted entrance hall after midnight, she slipped into the dark cloakroom and then into the toilet. The small window, through which she had squeezed several times before, was open, and in a few seconds she had clambered down onto the coal bunker below the window and run through the shrubbery and out of the back garden gate. Ten minutes later, she was sitting behind a secluded park bench in a large public garden overlooking the sea.

For some time, Triffy had been feeling unhappy and bored with life. She hated everybody – the bossy teacher who told her off in front of the class when she played truant, the pupils who laughed at her flaming red hair and freckly face, the girls in the dormitory who told tales on her, the staff who locked her up in the sickbay for two days when she was found wandering around the town at night, and the gang of loud-mouthed youths who hung around the esplanade after dark and often chased her, shouting rude words. All of them were out to get her.

Most of all, she resented the system which wouldn't permit her any freedom. Why couldn't she wander around the town alone for an hour or two? Her mum and dad had never worried about her going out whenever she liked. They had never pinned her down to mealtimes, or made her eat soggy sprouts or insisted she make her bed and tidy her drawers.

To be fair, Triffy had to admit that no one had been really unkind to her at the children's home. In fact, Mr Dawkin, the deputy warden, was quite a decent man who sometimes spoke up for her. On finding her for the second time in the park at two in the morning, he warned that if she absconded again, she would be sent to a much larger institution in Exeter where she would have even less freedom. 'You have to understand, Triffy, that we can't allow a ten-year-old to be walking around Sidmouth alone at night. If the police were to catch you, we would be in serious trouble.'

But the police will never catch me, thought Triffy gleefully. She was familiar with every inch of the town – the back lanes, the alleyways, the parks, the big hotel gardens, the harbour, the beach – all the places where a small nimble girl could safely hide. She had long since learnt how to avoid capture on her nocturnal escapades.

As far as Triffy was concerned, there were two words at the moment which summed up her life – *dead boring* – a phrase she had picked up from her father. In despair Mr Dawkin had remarked, 'You're a bright girl, Triffy. Why don't you find your lessons interesting?'

And she had replied annoyingly, ' 'Cos they're dead boring.'

'You're quite lucky to be in this children's home,' he had persisted. 'It's a lovely old house with a beautiful garden, and we do try to make life pleasant for you.'

'I haven't got any friends here and it's dead boring,' repeated Triffy.

'If you want friends, you have to be nice to people.'

'Why should I be nice to dead boring people?'

Mr Dawkin had lost patience and walked away.

On warm summer nights the live music, coloured lights, brightly lit shop windows and delicious aroma from the fast food bars, made Sidmouth seem a much more exciting place than during the day. Triffy enjoyed mingling with the holidaymakers on the seafront, listening to their chatter and staring at the teenagers in the latest fashion gear. But after midnight, when most of the tourists had returned to their hotels and guest houses, Triffy would sit on the front at the end of a great pile of chunky rocks with the sea lapping round her. She would stay there for an hour or more, confident that no one would spot her in the dark.

Mesmerised by the movement of the black water flecked with points of light from the hotel windows, her thoughts would turn to her dad. She still cherished a flicker of hope that he might rescue her from the children's home. She could conjure up his image quite clearly – the wide grin on his boyish face, the mop of unruly red hair just like her own, the teasing manner in which he told her jokes, the way he never asked awkward questions or seemed to worry about anything. Her mother, who had suffered from a long drawn-out illness, had constantly grumbled and shouted at Triffy, but her father had never scolded.

The three months after her mother's death, during which her dad had looked after her, had been a pleasant period in spite of the house being in a tip, the meals being few and far between and there not being enough money to pay all the bills. She had been allowed to wander around Sidmouth at all hours, and they had eaten fish and chips or a Chinese takeaway every day.

Occasionally on a Saturday, her father had taken her out on the back of his powerful motorbike. 'You and me's going for a spin, Triff,' he'd say. Then they'd race along the main road at a terrifying speed, to the seaside resort of Weymouth. On the way, Triffy had been aware of woods, fields, valleys and farms flashing by, but her father never stopped. 'The countryside's dead boring,' he said. Nothing interesting happened there. Far better to go to the pubs and cafés and amusement arcades in Weymouth. He'd buy his daughter ice cream and coke and once, a cheap ring with a circle of fake diamonds round a red glass stone.

One afternoon, her father had driven her a few miles along the coast, down steep winding lanes between high hedges of pink hawthorn blossom, to Branscombe, an age-old village. It was set amongst combes, where hills dipped into valleys and a network of secret grassy paths linked one remote farmhouse with another. 'We're going to visit your Gran,' he announced.

'Haven't I got a granddad?' asked Triffy.

'No, he died when I was a kid.'

They had driven down a long green valley dotted with sheep, and stopped outside a pink thatched cottage on a hill opposite a forge.

'Was this your home?' asked Triffy in amazement. She couldn't imagine her father living in a village.

'Yes, I went to primary school in Branscombe.'

'Did you like it here?'

Her father laughed. 'No, I couldn't get away soon enough.'

A woman with a stern expression opened the door. She wore ugly spectacles, and her iron-grey hair was wound round her head in a thick grey plait.

'Hello, Mum. I've brought your granddaughter, Triphena, to see you.'

The woman eyed them coldly and her mouth tightened. 'You needn't think to soften my heart, Ken Garland, by bringing your child here. When you deserted your wife and went to live with that blonde barmaid in Sidmouth, I was finished with you. I don't want to see you or your brat!'

As she spoke, Triffy heard an elderly quavering, but pleasant, voice in a room beyond the hallway. 'Who's there, Harriet?'

'No one you'd care to see, Mother.'

'Do bring your visitors in. I'd like to meet them.'

'They're not setting foot in my house, and there's an end to it.' Triffy was curious to see the old lady, but Mrs Garland shut the door firmly in their faces.

Triffy's father had grinned sheepishly and shrugged his shoulders, muttering, 'Crabby old cow!'

'Was that your Gran I heard?' enquired Triffy.

'Yes. She's been in a wheelchair for years. Gran's not a bad old bird. She used to stick up for me when I was a lad. Pity Mum wouldn't let us in.'

Then they had zoomed back up the lanes to Sidmouth.

On the last occasion her father had taken her to Weymouth, they had sat on the sand eating hotdogs, and he'd informed her that someone very special was coming to live with them. 'Sharon's a great girl, Triff. I hope you'll get on together.'

But they hadn't got on at all. Triffy lost no time in telling her dad's girlfriend what she thought of her, and after a fortnight, Sharon had said, 'It's me or the kid, Ken. Make your choice.'

So Triffy was told she'd have to go into a children's home. 'Only for a few months,' said her father soothingly. But those months had stretched into years, and during that time he had never come to visit her. The superintendent said her dad had moved to Plymouth, and it was too far for him to travel to Sidmouth.

After thinking about her father as she sat on the rocks, Triffy's mind would go over her present life in the children's home. Outwardly she always put on a rebellious, *I don't care, I want to be different,* attitude. But inwardly, she often did want to join in with the other girls, who talked mainly about boyfriends, make-up, clothes, horror videos, rave-ups and drugs, and listened to loud, brain-shattering music. She had even streaked her short red hair with green dye to be in fashion, but no one was impressed. She wanted to be liked, to have a special friend, or to join a gang, but she had never quite fitted in and had resigned herself to being a loner.

It was only late at night, crouched amongst the dark rocks, listening to the sea swishing up and down the shingle, that Triffy had thoughts of quite a different kind. She imagined what might be at the bottom of the sea, or above the sky, or beyond the horizon. She wondered about all the people who had ever lived in the world and wished she could leave her body for a while and float away to meet some of them. She kept hoping she might see ghosts from past centuries. The idea didn't frighten her; it just made delicious shivers run down her back.

She thought she might have been happier living in a different age. She invented a big friendly family for herself, the kind of family she had once seen on television, in old-fashioned costumes, sitting beside a log fire or sharing a home-cooked meal by candlelight on a table covered with a gleaming white cloth. In those days, she was sure, children didn't get dumped into institutions unless they were orphans. If only she could disappear from her own unsatisfactory life and reappear in another, more interesting one. She would shut her eyes and let her mind go blank and then wish hard to open them and find herself somewhere else. But it had never worked. She was stuck in Sidmouth and it would be time for her to slip back to the dormitory without being detected.

Tonight, however, she had escaped for good. As a distant clock struck one, she wondered if her empty bed had been discovered and whether Mr Dawkin was already out searching for her. She needed the hours of darkness to rest and to decide exactly what she was going to do at dawn. Her plan was to go to Branscombe to find her grandmother. It probably wouldn't be much fun living in the country, but she knew of no other relatives. Her Gran hadn't wanted to see her, but maybe when she described how awful it was living in the children's home, the old lady might be sorry and take her in.

CHAPTER 2

As the hot, still night crept by, and the park seemed to become darker and even a little spooky, Triffy began to feel intensely lonely. If only she had a friend to share her forthcoming adventure. The thought of leaving Sidmouth and venturing into the huge and unknown countryside, all by herself, seemed scary and uncertain. What would be the best way to go to Branscombe? She had never been out of Sidmouth on foot, and knew nothing of the surrounding area, but there was a tourist map on the seafront showing a coast path all the way to Branscombe. Hikers carrying heavy backpacks, were often seen coming down the steps from the towering red cliff above the bay at the eastern end of the town. She didn't fancy the long, hard slog up that cliff, and it might take her more than a day to reach her destination along the path. The idea of a night alone on top of a cliff didn't appeal, but if she were to go by road, a police car might spot her. It would be safer to take the coast path. Yet how could she undertake such a strenuous walk in her flimsy sandals? Better to risk the road and hitch a lift. One of the older boys at the children's home had assured her it was easy to hitch a lift. He had once spent five days hitching lifts. 'You just stick your arm out and wave it in the right direction and sooner or later a car will stop,' he had said.

The night wore on until the sky was rosy with the light of the unrisen sun. Before setting out, Triffy knew she must find something to eat. As the sun appeared at the start of another sweltering day, she walked cautiously to the seafront where flocks of goose-like cormorants were gathering with outstretched wings on the reddish pebbles. There was no one about, so she was able to inspect the overflowing litter bins. Soon she had acquired three half-finished packets of crisps, a cheese roll, some soggy chips, half a chocolate bar and a tin of coke.

She gobbled down the roll and the chocolate and drank a few mouthfuls from a public drinking fountain. Feeling much stronger, she hurried along the river to the main road, and then turned off to begin the trek up Salcombe Hill. She had never walked up this very steep road before, and by the time she passed the last of the houses and reached the ancient woodland high above the town, she was exhausted by the heat. And so far, not a single car had overtaken her.

Collapsing onto a thick carpet of dry leaves, she drank all the water in her plastic bottle. *How long would it take to walk to Branscombe?* she wondered. *And how would she manage without another drink?* Already her mouth was dry and her tee shirt was soaked with sweat. *Would a car ever come up this way and give her a lift?* Half an hour later, to her great relief, she heard a car pulling up the hill. Leaping to her feet, she began to wave. A large estate car with a canoe fixed on the roof, drew up beside her. A couple were sitting in the front, with two small boys in the back. 'Where are you heading for?' asked the father.

'Branscombe.'

'Hop in, then. We can take you to Branscombe.'

One of the boys opened the car door and Triffy sank thankfully onto the comfortable rear seat. How easy it had been to thumb a lift, and how thrilling to be riding in a car for the first time. Behind her was piled a heap of plastic bags full of provisions, together with a crate of beer. She felt safe enough, for this was just an ordinary family returning from the supermarket. 'We're on holiday at Weston,' explained the mother, 'and it's not far from there to Branscombe.'

The car speeded up and Triffy thought cheerfully, *Soon I'll be in Branscombe and I'll find my gran and maybe my great-gran, and they'll let me live with them...*

'What's your name?' asked one of the boys.

When she told him the father exclaimed heartily, 'Triphena! What an unusual name. How pretty!'

'How very pretty!' echoed the mother.

Instead of driving straight to Branscombe, the car stopped outside Ash Grove Caravan Park at the top of Weston Combe.

'As it's so hot,' said the father, 'I think we'd better unload the shopping and put it in the fridge. I expect you could do with a drink, Triphena, before I take you on to Branscombe.'

As they drove through the gate, Triffy noticed a signpost pointing down towards the thickly wooded valley. It read: 'Branscombe & Sidmouth. Link to South-West Coast Path'. It was very quiet on the site, since everyone had gone down to the sea to cool off in the heat. The family carried the shopping to their large, luxury mobile home set very pleasantly amongst trees, not too close to the other caravans. Inside it was hot and stuffy. The two boys stripped off their shirts and hurried outside, while the mother disappeared into the kitchen. She poured a beer for her husband and a lemonade for Triffy, before going out to keep an eye on her children.

Triffy sat down at the table opposite the father and for the first time, she became aware of just how tall and well-built he was, and how large and strong his hands were. When he smiled, his white teeth looked too perfect. As he sipped his beer, he asked whether she was expected home to lunch.

'No,' she replied, hoping he wouldn't ask any more questions. There was something about his eyes she didn't like. The more he smiled at her, the more uncomfortable she felt.

Suddenly, she knew she must escape from that caravan.

The man got up, saying, 'Well, Triphena, I'll just rinse the glasses and then we'll be on our way.' Now was her chance, but as she was deciding whether to run along the lane or to go down to the coast path, the man emerged from the kitchen.

'Right, let's go.' He descended the caravan steps to the car and opened the passenger door for her. In that instant, Triffy made a dash down the valley, trusting in her ability to sprint fast enough to get well ahead and out of sight so she could hide in the woods.

The man called, 'Hey! Where are you going?' And immediately she was being chased along a ridged concrete track. Finding it impossible to keep up any speed in her flimsy sandals, she allowed them to slip off and continued barefoot. The route soon forked and she took a rough stony track descending steeply to the left. Without glancing back, Triffy plunged down a bank to conceal herself in a thicket of bushes and overhanging ash trees. She lay on the ground breathing hard and desperately hoping her pursuer hadn't seen her leave the main track.

A few seconds later she heard him shouting, 'Come back, you silly girl! No one's going to hurt you.'

But Triffy remained in hiding until eventually, she heard the man walking back. Poking her head a little way out of the foliage, she noticed he was carrying her sandals. This was a blow. She had meant to retrace her steps and retrieve them. How was she to walk all the way to Branscombe without shoes? Already one of her toes was bleeding, and when she began to move along the stony track each step was agony. Perhaps she had acted too hastily. Maybe the man was just being kind. All she knew was that she had never felt so scared in anyone's presence before, and how mean, mean, mean of him to take her sandals!

CHAPTER 3

Triffy hobbled painfully over the sharp stones until she reached a gate, beyond which lay a wide grassy track, which soon gave way to more stony ground. *If this goes on*, she thought, *I'll take a week to reach Branscombe.* Fortunately, after hopping over a second stile, she found herself at the bottom of a huge sloping field. A narrow path on soft ground ran parallel to a stream trickling down a gully on her left, protected by a barbed wire fence. Now that the walking was much easier, Triffy was able to look about her. On the banks of the stream, grew tall showy clumps of willowherb with small rose-coloured flowers and hairy leaves. On either side of the valley, a blanket of green rose to the top of towering cliffs. Triffy felt very lost amidst all this unfamiliar nature. It was so quiet, and she longed to be back on the noisy streets of Sidmouth.

As she stood gazing up at the cliff she had to climb, without warning a deer appeared from the undergrowth and bounded effortlessly up a steep triangular field covered in tall yellow ragwort on the west side of the valley. Triffy was entranced by her first sight of an animal in the wild and for the moment forgot her fears. If only she could move up the cliff like that deer!

At the next stile, she discovered that the path now descended an almost vertical cliff face down to Weston beach. To her dismay she realised there was no path bridging the stream, because the gully had become a steep, wide ravine at

11

this point. If she was to continue up the east cliff towards Branscombe, she would have to go all the way down to the beach to cross the stream. Luckily, steps had been fashioned in the hardened red soil, edged with sturdy lengths of pine, to make the descent easier.

She went down these uneven steps very gingerly in her bare feet. A profusion of colourful wild flowers grew on the sunny open cliff face, all combining to produce a heady sweet aroma in the heat. None of the plants was known to Triffy, who could barely recognise anything more than a daisy or a dandelion, but she thought they were quite pretty.

Groups of sunbathers were spread out along the lengthy shingle, but no one took any notice of Triffy. A light breeze was coming off the sea and she would dearly have liked to swim, but there was no time to lose; she had to move on to Branscombe. After crossing the stream trickling over the pebbles into the sea, she was unable at first to find a path up the eastern cliff, but at last she discovered a signpost beside a red buoy hanging on a post.

If she'd realised how long and exhausting a climb lay ahead of her she would certainly have taken a rest. As it was, the journey up many steps, across an enormous field, along twisting paths, through thickets of bramble and hawthorn and tall clumps of sorrel and wild carrot – always leading up and yet further up – brought her near to collapsing in the heat long before she reached the summit. Why had she attempted the coast path? She had never bargained for such difficult terrain. How she loathed this countryside with no people and no shops. Yet the desire to reach Branscombe before nightfall kept her going.

At the peak, she flopped down onto a tussock of brittle grass, dried almost white by the blazing sun and the wind. Far, far below, lay the wide blue bay. Her head was throbbing and she felt faint. The light stabbed at her eyes and her vision became obscured by a sheet of hazy red fog. She lay back and placed her hands over her face, but the unrelenting sun penetrated her eyelids, sending flashes of colour across the aching blackness.

The atmosphere became unnaturally quiet, like the lull before a storm, and suddenly she heard a loud gasp of surprise directly overhead, followed by soft girlish laughter and then, more distantly, the braying of a donkey. Startled, she leapt up and looked around. Her eyes took a while to focus, but there was no one in sight. Several black-backed gulls were screeching in the sky and a motorboat was chugging across the bay, but there was definitely no movement on the cliff. Had she really heard laughter and the noise of a donkey, or had it been a dream?

With a shudder, she observed how close to the edge of the cliff she was standing. A few posts and snapped off strands of barbed wire afforded no real protection. She gazed down at the pristine white shingle with its darker edge at the drift line, and then across the valley at the great sculptured slabs of weathered vertical rock comprising the cliff face. But just now, she had no interest in the view. Feeling weak and dizzy, she dropped down again onto the grass.

She devoured the soggy chips, gulped down the coke and recovered a little. Then she rose to continue her journey across the desiccated grass, along the level top of the cliffs. The path skirted two long fields on her left, where a notice pinned to a post stated that the first field had been set aside for the protection of wild flowers. This stretch of coast was a habitat for several rare plants, including a flower named blue gromwell – otherwise only to be found in parts of Somerset and Wales. *What an odd name*, she thought. *Why would wild flowers need protecting?*

On the seaward side of the path, only a hedge of thorn bushes mixed with patches of tall prickly teasel, stood between Triffy and a treacherous drop down the cliff. Keeping well away from the edge she pursued her endless walk over another stile, down a sward of grassland sloping towards a wide shallow vale and then across more expanses of short turf stretching along the verge of the cliff. Cows, sheep and a farm could be seen in the distance, but still no people, till unexpectedly she came across half a dozen cars parked on the grass, near which families were picnicking.

The fizzy drink had made Triffy feel sick, and she sat down to rest with her head between her knees, a picture of misery with her bleeding feet, grubby clothes and scratched arms and legs. Presently a woman approached, exclaiming, 'You poor child, whatever's happened to you?'

'I fell over coming up the cliff,' lied Triffy quickly.

'But why aren't you wearing shoes?'

'The tide carried them away while I was swimming.'

'Come over to our car, and I'll put some antiseptic lotion and plasters on those cuts. I think there's a pair of old trainers in the boot that might fit you.'

Triffy had no desire to become involved again with a stranger, but the thought of acquiring some footwear, impelled her to follow the woman. Lotion and plasters were administered and a pair of trainers produced – too large, but better than nothing.

'Where do you live, my dear?' asked the woman.

'Branscombe.'

'I could drive you home if you like.'

'Oh no,' said Triffy hastily, 'I can easily walk. Thanks for the shoes.' And she hurried away.

But she still felt sick and had to sit down again behind a copse of gorse. For the first time since starting on her journey, she had misgivings about finding her grandmother. *What if she's moved? What if she sends me away because I look so scruffy?* A couple of small boys passed close by and turned to point in her direction, giggling at her over-large shoes and the green tufts still growing out in her red hair. Then a toddler ran up and stared. There was to be no peace. People would not leave her alone and yet she had no strength to carry on in the heat without a long rest and a drink. If only she'd accepted that offer of a lift into Branscombe!

Nearby, she noticed a lone post sticking up out of the turf. Beneath the carving of an acorn, was painted a fat yellow arrow pointing down towards the sea. On looking more closely, she discovered an unobtrusive path disappearing steeply onto a cliff face, thickly covered with bushes and trees. If she were to venture down this shady route, she might find a cool place to rest undisturbed.

In the large uncomfortable trainers, Triffy picked her way carefully down the hard uneven ground. Within a yard or two, she was astonished to discover a small rusting iron gate such as she had often seen at the entrance to small gardens in Sidmouth. Beyond the gate, in contrast to the sunlit cliff top, the path plunged into a shadowy, mysterious jungle of twisted trees and long creepers. Climbing plants interlocked above her head in festoons, while long brambles caught savagely at her legs. Underfoot, lichen, moss and ferns spread a moist emerald carpet over tree roots and small rocks. Away from the path, hardly any of the ground seemed to be accessible. To her intense disappointment, instead of being cooler, Triffy found this wooded cliff face unbearably humid. The air was stagnant and heavy, worse than anything she had ever experienced.

She flopped down on a flat stone in the steamy atmosphere, feeling intimidated by the silence. Although she wasn't far from where people were picnicking, it felt as though she had suddenly been cut off from civilisation, as though these woods existed beyond time and place. She wanted to escape back to the open ground, and she was desperate for water, but she lacked the power to move.

The quiet was broken by the loud hollow drumming of a woodpecker, and soon she became aware that there were other sounds to be heard in the stillness. The air was resonant with the hum of unseen insects and the faint rustlings of hidden animals. Then a dead branch fell with a crash. She strained her ears and thought she could hear the sound of trickling water. In excitement she rose, determined to find a way to reach it.

Working her way cautiously over the rocky terrain, she reached a parting of ways, where a second yellow arrow on a post directed her downwards. Listening intently once again, it seemed that the sound of water came from below, so she followed the way straight down, alongside a deep dark chasm, choked with trees, creepers and towering firs. The path bent sharply leftwards just below a ruined hut, and then plunged down again, before giving Triffy another choice of ways – up or down. Now she could hear the water above her, and she started climbing. In her desperation to procure a drink she hurtled along, almost tripping several times, until suddenly there it was – a spring gushing out of a pipe onto a glistening flat rock. Triffy lay on the ground on her back and placed her hot, flushed face under the cold flow, letting the water run into her mouth and down her neck. Such delicious relief!

She rested awhile, drank again, and much invigorated, rose to her feet. Perhaps after all, she might reach Branscombe before evening. Then she noticed subsidiary paths to the left and the right of the main path, each leading to a wooden chalet perched on a level plateau of undercliff, surrounded by a well-tended garden, bounded by a hedge with a gate. One chalet bore the quaint name *Elbow Room*, and the other *Bag End*. Triffy was astonished to find this evidence of human habitation.

Continuing upwards, yet another signpost guided her eastwards along the top of the undercliff. High above, she could see a grassy chalk overhang and ahead more chalets, one named *The Eyrie*. She reached four steps going down, and then a fork in the path and a triangle of ash trees. At this point, a breeze off the sea carried a faint but definite odour of barbecued meat to her nostrils. If she had continued straight on she would soon have emerged from this strange wooded cliff and found herself on a track to Branscombe. As it was, the effort of the day had made her exceedingly hungry, and the idea of food drove her down the cliff towards the tantalising smell.

For part of the way, an orange plastic rope attached to a couple of wobbly iron posts, aided her descent. Then came a series of hairpin bends traversing ground which was slashed by deep ravines running alongside the precariously narrow path. Triffy tacked her way down, constantly stumbling, and once slithering dangerously, on a permanent muddy patch caused by an underground spring. Soon she was aching all over, and her body felt like a lead weight in the heat. This kind of walking was very far removed from nipping in and out of alleyways in Sidmouth. Towards the bottom, Triffy encountered several entry paths to chalets in their tiny secret gardens.

So far, she had seen no sign of life in any of the chalets, but suddenly she found herself looking down on a large, freshly painted green and white chalet built on a wide plateau a few feet above the beach. A pink rambler rose ran riot over the door and round the windows, scattering some of its petals into a large yellow water butt.

A couple of men with massive hairy chests and lobster-coloured bellies bulging over satin swimming trunks, were seated beside a barbecue on a verandah, talking to two women in bikinis with dyed platinum hair and dark glasses. A rustic table was laden with tins of beer, bottles of sauce, a platter of sizzling sausages, a bowl of fried onion rings and a basket of long bread rolls.

A small lawn lay in front of the chalet and two gnarled apple trees loaded with unripe fruit, grew out of the narrow strip of soil at the back. Triffy proceeded slowly and quietly down towards the chalet until she reached a white gate on which the name *Sea Vista* was painted in gothic lettering. She moved back up the path and hid behind the chalet. From here she could just see a large motorboat anchored in the bay close to the shore. She waited for twenty minutes, not sure of what she intended to do, but the smell of those sausages acted like a magnet. Then, miracle of miracles, she watched all four occupants going down to the beach, carrying towels. She entered the open gate, and had no qualms whatsoever about helping herself to a sausage, and then gobbling down a second, a third and a fourth. There were so many, who would miss them? Finally, she slipped half a dozen rolls into her rucksack and turned to flee.

At that moment, a whitish-grey bull terrier emerged from the chalet and threw itself at her, snarling ferociously and knocking her to the ground. It stood over her, dripping saliva onto her tee shirt, its claws digging painfully into her arm.

Alerted by the barking, one of the men hurried up from the beach and yelled, 'Release!' and reluctantly, the dog let go. The man spotted the open rucksack full of rolls, and bellowed, 'You thieving young devil! I've a good mind to hand you over to the police for theft and trespass. Now beat it, or my dog will have you for supper. And don't ever show your face down here again.'

Triffy moved as fast as possible, until her persecutors were out of sight behind the first hairpin bend. Then it became an endurance test to keep one foot going in front of the other. Her terror in the face of the savage dog had sapped away what vestige remained of her energy, and it was all she could do to stand upright.

The sun became trapped behind a bank of thin cloud and a warm sea mist began to creep in amongst the trees. The woods darkened and Triffy could barely see the way. She was no longer climbing. The path was leading her sideways to another spring, and then to her despair, downwards again into a shadowy gorge. The next moment her feet were in water and she had bumped her head against a fallen tree. There may have been a path once, but now the land had slipped away and there was nothing ahead but rocky jungle. She struggled back to the spring, and cupping her hands she managed to drink and splash her face. Then sinking down among the mossy stones she burst into tears. Why had she ever come to this dreadful place? *If I can't get off the cliff by sunset,* she thought, *I'll have to spend the night here alone. What if that vicious dog is allowed to run loose?* In such a frightening wood she could believe in evil spirits keeping her imprisoned in this enchanted spot for ever.

In a while, however, the sun burnt off the mist draped over the cliff. Light began to penetrate the foliage and once more Triffy was able to see her surroundings. She was sitting in a small copse of tall bamboo shoots, intermingled with pink and orange flowers, which looked more like cultivated, than wild flowers. Butterflies were alighting on the dark purple of buddleia, the magenta of fuchsia and the blue of hebe, and high above her the white lacy blooms of an Asian vine cascaded over a bent tree growing out of a rock. Fearing that if she had stumbled into someone's garden, a person or a dog might appear, she dragged herself up and found the way back to the main path. She concentrated on walking eastwards until all at once, she emerged from the woodland and found herself treading on soft green rabbit-bitten turf. The beach could be seen far below, its long surf stretching into the distance. The air was still warm and heavy, and beyond the shingle, the sea resembled a sheet of shining metal. A weird molten-orange sun hung over the cliffs towards Sidmouth.

The grassy path ran roughly straight, passing a few overhanging chalk rocks covered with a tangle of discoloured ivy. Beneath them, to her surprise, she found a sturdy wooden seat close to the edge of the cliff. Carved upon its back were the words 'Eli's Seat'. She sat down wondering who Eli might have been. Out of the woods she felt less frightened, and in normal circumstances it might have been very pleasant sitting here in the late afternoon looking out to sea. But now, how tired she was, how very tired! When she lay down using her rucksack as a pillow, it felt too hard. Much better to lie on the grass beside the seat.

Stretched out more comfortably on the ground, she became aware of miniature flowers at eye level – plants she would never have noticed when standing upright. She had no idea such tiny flowers existed, and each one fashioned so exquisitely. She gazed at white eyebright tinged with mauve and marked with a yellow spot, blue milkwort with its unusual fringed petals, yellow stonecrop with its mat of tiny reddish leaves and two tiny dog-violets in a tuft of heart-shaped leaves. She fell asleep, marvelling for the first time in her life at the beauty of a flower.

CHAPTER 4

She woke just before dusk, feeling stiff and distinctly chilly. She could hear voices, and raising her head a little, she noted with horror that two men were sitting above her. Their hobnailed boots could be seen under the seat. They must have seen her asleep on the grass, and yet they were talking as if she wasn't there.

'Been a bad day for I,' said one of the men. 'Most o' that new soil at the bottom of my plat rolled down when I were digging it in, and I spent an hour carrying it up again.'

'That's happened to I afore now. What can us expect on a cliff face? If us had a big level plat like Davey, 'twould be a sight easier.'

'Have you seen Davey's donkey? I reckon that poor creature'll be dead afore summer.'

'Shouldn't be surprised if Phena drops dead too. Such a pale, thin little 'un! You'd never guess she were eleven years old. 'Tis wicked the way Jack lets his daughter be driven by Davey. Three trips she's made to Weston today.'

'Trouble is, Jack's always done as Davey tells 'e. 'E could never stand up to his brother.'

'I've no time for Jack or Davey Edgecombe. Jack's a coward, and Davey's a bully. Nellie says Davey drove old Harry off his plat by threatening to poison his donkey. 'E's a troublemaker and us ought to try and get shot of 'e.'

'They say 'e's thinking of emigrating to Canada. Sooner the better, I say.'

There was a short silence, and Triffy's nose filled with the pungent smell of lit tobacco.

'Two hundred bunches of anemones I sold in Sidmouth today. Four inches across mine are this spring.'

'That path along Kill Ground's drying out at last.'

''Bout time. Never known such a wet April. Snails is already at my flowers.'

'You'll never get rid of they on the plats. It's the chalk. They like it for their shells.'

'Do they now? I never thought of that. You coming down for a drop of slag wine?'

'No, I must get home. Wife'll be waiting.'

All the time the men were chatting, Triffy was thinking, *In a moment they'll see me and start asking awkward questions.* But the men rose from the seat and walked past her without a glance. It was only then she observed they were wearing rather old-fashioned clothes – corduroy breeches held up by braces, dark brown leggings tied under the knee, thick striped collarless shirts under their waistcoats, and shabby peaked caps.

This incident was more unnerving than her experience in the caravan park. She shivered in the cold evening air, wondering how the weather could have changed so suddenly. It was really frightening. What had she seen, and what more might she see when darkness fell? There was no longer any question of sleeping beside the seat.

As she sat rigid with apprehension, wondering what she might do next, the atmosphere warmed up again, and there came a distant sound of jazz music. The way ahead looked impenetrable but she ventured on, almost bent double, ducking under merciless bramble, shoving overgrown bushes and low branches aside, and constantly tripping over obtrusive stones. The path twisted and turned, sometimes affording her a view of the sea through a tracery of ash leaves. Once her foot slipped down a gully, and only with extreme difficulty did she avoid losing her shoe. Eventually, almost fainting with fatigue, she reached a fork in the path and followed the music down to the right. Turning a corner, she saw a wooden gate from which hung an open padlock on a heavy chain. The name, *Davey's linhay*, was carved in varnished wood along the top. Through a dense hedge of blackthorn encased in bindweed, clematis and honeysuckle, Triffy could make out lighted flares in a garden. Judging by the music, the loud voices and the laughter, a party was going on outside.

Triffy walked through the gate and saw the outline of a large chalet in the dusk. There were no lights on, since the owners and their guests were sitting on a terrace at the seaward end of the garden. She knew she would be courting trouble if she entered the chalet, but her fear of spending the night alone on the cliff overcame her fear of being discovered. It was so comforting just to be near ordinary human beings after encountering the strange men on the seat.

She crept across the paving stones to the open door of the chalet and slipped inside. Her eyes were already used to the dark, and she was able to see she was in a living room. Dropping her rucksack onto the floor, she sank down onto a long sofa and kicked off her trainers. She lay back against the soft cushions, thinking, *I'll just take a little rest and then move before someone finds me.* But she was so exhausted she no longer cared. All that mattered was sleep, a long deep sleep.

CHAPTER 5

Triffy woke just before dawn, feeling cold again. It was pitch-black and claustrophobic. She was no longer lying on a sofa, but on a thin hard mattress under a coarse hairy blanket. Discovering with relief that her rucksack was still beside her, she unfastened it and felt for her torch. Flashing it round the walls she found she was in a very small room. It could just accommodate two narrow bunk beds with a small chest in-between, on which stood a candlestick and a white jug in a matching bowl. A nightdress with long sleeves and a high neck, together with a woollen cloak lined with flannel, hung from pegs on the wooden walls. There was no rug on the rough floorboards. It was like being in a large, musty cupboard. Then with a shock, she saw that someone had carved the name *Triphena* in large, neat capital letters several times on the wall alongside the other bed.

Where was she, and who had put her here? How did they know her name? Unlike the evening before, she was more puzzled than frightened at finding herself in this mystifying situation. If she were to try and leave this room, where would she find herself?

Birds were starting to sing outside and the room lightened somewhat as though the dawn was trying to come in. Triffy sat up and pulled the blanket round her shoulders waiting for what might happen next. Then, very quietly, the door opened.

Triffy's body stiffened on seeing a person standing in the doorway. In the grey light issuing from a window let into the roof of the adjoining room, Triffy could make out a girl smiling sweetly at her – a small slender girl, no taller than herself, with a thick auburn plait hanging over one shoulder. It was hard to guess the girl's age, for in spite of her diminutive size, her face looked mature and there were already fine lines under her eyes. Triffy could see she was clad in clothes from another period – a threadbare high-necked blouse in a coarse cream material and a worn ankle-length skirt with two large sagging pockets. The slightly elongated face, the large dark eyes, high cheekbones, sallow skin and full red lips, reminded Triffy of an old-fashioned oil painting she had seen in a shop window. Even the sad, sweet smile looked out of date, yet this apparition was in no way frightening.

'You're still here,' observed the girl softly, shutting the door. 'I was afeard you might be gone.' She spoke so naturally and in such a good-humoured tone, as though it hadn't surprised her in the least to find a stranger in her bedroom. ''Tis a hard bed,' the girl continued in a whisper, 'I wonder you slept at all.'

'I was very tired,' Triffy whispered back.

'I have to rise before dawn. When I lit my candle, there you were.'

'Do your family live in this horrible dark hut?' asked Triffy bluntly.

'Yes. It's a linhay with a wall built onto the front and a shed on each side. I live here with my father, Jack Edgecombe, and his brother, Davey.'

'What's your name?'

'Triphena, but they call me Phena.'

Triffy felt a tingle down her spine. She had always imagined herself to be the only girl with such an outlandish name. 'That's my name too. I'm Triffy for short.'

Phena stared at Triffy for a moment and then remarked, 'You do look a strange sight with those bits of green hair, and clothes that hardly cover you.'

'You look just as peculiar in your old-fashioned things with those awful black buttoned boots!' retorted Triffy.

'The girls in Branscombe have better clothes than mine, but I don't need good clothes to work in.'

'How did I get to this hut?'

Phena laughed and said in a matter-of-fact voice, 'You're a ghost. My mother could see into the future. She said I might have the same gift.'

Triffy was taken aback. 'I'm not a ghost!' she cried indignantly. 'You can only become a ghost after you've died.'

'You're a ghost from the future.'

'That's rubbish!' insisted Triffy rudely. 'I live in Sidmouth and I'm not a ghost. In fact, you must be the ghost, because you come from the past.'

But Phena's assertion was not to be shaken. 'Which year are you living in?' she asked.

'1994.'

'1994! How amazing. Well, you've come to the year 1912. You've come as a ghost from the future to my life. Not me to yours.'

'How can anyone be a ghost from the future?' said Triffy, but inside herself she wasn't so sure. Certainly something very mysterious had happened to her.

'I had a dream about you,' said Phena. 'You were sitting on the rocks at night in Sidmouth. Then, yesterday I was coming home with Topsy, our donkey, when I saw you, just for a moment, lying at the top of Weston Cliff, asleep.'

Triffy recalled the girlish laughter and the braying, and felt uncomfortable. 'How could you have seen me?'

'I don't understand it myself. It just happened. When I saw your strange clothes I knew you'd come from a different time. You disappeared and I was sorry and wished you could stay.'

'What for?' asked Triffy, disliking the idea that someone might have some kind of magical power over her.

'Because I need a friend, and you looked about my age,' replied Phena simply.

'You can't be friends with a ghost.'

'Why not? It's better than no friend at all.'

'How do you know I want to be your friend?'

'When I saw you in my dream on the rocks, you looked so lonely. I thought perhaps like me, you needed a friend.'

'Whatever's happened to me, I'm certainly not a ghost,' said Triffy firmly.

'Listen,' said Phena, 'when I woke this morning I heard breathing. I lit my candle and saw you lying on that bed, but when I came to touch your shoulder to wake you I couldn't feel your body.'

Triffy was stunned.

'Now see if you can feel my hand,' said Phena.

Triffy grasped the hand held out to her and felt the rough skin over the girl's delicate bones. 'I can't feel *your* fingers. I can only see them,' said Phena.

Triffy shuddered. *Had she died in the chalet and become a disembodied spirit, an outline with no substance?*

'It's nothing to worry about,' said Phena kindly. 'Of course you're a real person in the future, but here in my life, you're a ghost. You'll probably be able to walk through closed doors and you'll be invisible to everyone but me.'

This is just a bad dream, thought Triffy. *In a minute I'll wake up in the holiday chalet.*

Phena sat on the edge of the bed looking so friendly and normal that Triffy felt calmer.

'Now you've come, will you stay for a while and be my friend?'

'I might not like being in your life.'

'No, it's a hard life. If you want to go, I'll not stop you.' Tears stood in Phena's dark eyes and for the first time, Triffy experienced the pleasure of being wanted as a friend. 'I'll stay for the moment,' she conceded, though she had no choice in the matter.

CHAPTER 6

'You'll have to remember that no one can see or hear you apart from me. I won't be able to speak to you in front of my father or my uncle or anyone else, or they'll think I'm mad. It won't be easy at first, but we'll get used to it. I'll bring you some breakfast in here.'

She went into the main room and returned with a bowl of steaming porridge which Triffy gulped down, too hungry to mind that there was no milk or sugar in it. After she had finished, she put on her scruffy trainers.

'What strange shoes,' said Phena.

'All the kids wear trainers in my life.'

'We can't talk any more now because I have to go and work for my uncle.'

'What do you do?'

'I milk our goat and feed the hens. If we need it, I go down to the beach to collect driftwood for the stove. Then my father and I fill the panniers with teddies and load them onto our donkey.'

'Teddies? D'you mean teddy bears?' asked Triffy in surprise.

Phena placed her hand over her mouth to stop herself laughing. 'No, of course not. Teddies are the new potatoes we grow. My uncle rents two pieces of land on this cliff. They're called plats. We grow potatoes and other vegetables here at the linhay, and anemones and strawberries on the plat lower down the cliff. During the season, I take them to a farm at Weston and once a week to Sidmouth market.'

'How do you get there?'

'I walk with our donkey, of course.'

'All the way to Sidmouth and back?' Triffy was astounded.

'It's only hard in bad weather. Come into the kitchen now. I have to give the men their breakfast.'

Triffy followed Phena into the adjoining room. A kerosene lamp stood on a scrubbed table spattered with candle grease. Two heavy iron saucepans and an iron kettle stood on a blackened iron range kept going with logs in a firebox. A flitch of bacon hung from a beam across the roof, and sacks of grain and potatoes were stacked in a corner. A cupboard, a couple of benches, a stool and an assortment of rough shelves completed the furniture. Triffy noticed with distaste that the floor consisted of packed earth. *Only fit for animals*, she thought. It was an utterly dismal room, with nothing to relieve its drabness.

Phena went to stir the rest of the porridge, saying quietly, 'Sit on that stool till I'm ready to go outside.'

Then the door on the opposite side of the kitchen opened and two dark-haired men entered, dressed in much the same style as those sitting on Eli's Seat the day before. Triffy guessed that probably the small, bony anaemic-looking man, with watery bloodshot eyes and a persistent cough, was Phena's father, Jack. His brother, Davey, was a big, bearded character with a sunburnt complexion and hard round eyes the colour of damsons. He immediately began to scold Phena.

'Better stop that foolishness, my girl.'

'What foolishness, Uncle?'

'That talking to yourself. 'Tis time you grew up.'

'I've no one else to talk to while I'm working.'

'Nor have I, but I don't go round gabbling away like a maniac. People in the village will think you're soft in the head, or bewitched like your mother.' Davey sat down heavily on a bench and tied the laces of his huge boots. 'And hurry up with that porridge.'

When the men had finished their breakfast, Davey said 'You'd better get going, and no dawdling. No stopping to look at flowers. The teds will be ready by seven.'

Triffy found it hard to believe that the men couldn't see her. It was just as well, for she had taken an instant dislike to both of them. She judged Jack to be weak-spirited, with no mind of his own. What a depressing thought, to live with men like these! How on earth could Phena stand it?

Phena went back into her room and Triffy followed. 'Have you anything warm to wear over your shirt?'

'Isn't it hot outside?'

'No, not yet. It's still spring.'

Triffy pulled her cardigan out of the rucksack. Phena flung a shawl over her shoulders and then put on a heavy cotton goffered bonnet, with pointed flaps coming down over her ears.

'What a peculiar hat!' remarked Triffy, giggling.

'It is a bit old-fashioned. It was my mother's.'

On the way out of the linhay, Phena picked up a large stout basket with leather straps to enable her to carry it on her back.

'What time is it?' asked Triffy.

'Half past five.'

'Why d'you have to get up so early?'

'To get a good day's work done.'

Outside, Triffy could see that Phena's home occupied the same plot of land as the chalet she'd fallen asleep in. The two bedrooms were lean-to extensions under a roof of wooden shingles. Instead of a lawn and a flower garden, the half-acre plot was given over to the growing of vegetables in well-weeded beds. Phena led the way to the back of the linhay where the goat and the donkey were tethered in a large shed. Attached to the shed was a hen house and a primitive toilet consisting of a hole in the ground between two planks. Triffy was disgusted.

'Davey refuses to build a better toilet, so we have to make do,' explained Phena.

'I'm not using it!' said Triffy.

'You can go off and find a place in the woods, and as you're invisible you'll be quite safe.' Triffy was relieved at this prospect.

Phena sat on a stool to milk Izzy, the goat, into a pail. Triffy was fascinated but didn't fancy the job.

'I didn't know you could drink goat's milk.'

'Goat's milk is richer than cow's milk. We get about a gallon a day and sell it at a penny a jugful.'

'What does your goat eat?'

'Oats, mainly.' Phena poured the frothing milk from a pail into a churn and left it standing at the back of the shed.

'I suppose you don't have a fridge?' said Triffy.

'What's a fridge?'

'A sort of white box worked by electricity, that keeps everything cold.'

'When it's very hot on the plats in the summer we just have to drink the milk quickly.'

Phena took a bag down from a shelf and scattered some grain for the hens to peck up. 'When our hens are laying well we sell the eggs, twenty for a shilling.'

'What's a shilling?' asked Triffy.

'There are twelve pennies in a shilling – don't you know that?'

'Our money is different. Why is your vegetable garden called a plat?'

'It's just a name. Some of the cliff farmers call their gardens ledges, but mostly they're known as the plats. You'll see plats of all shapes and sizes on this cliff. Some are easier to work than others. Davey has his second plat halfway down, where he grows anemones. Follow me.'

Phena led Triffy a short way back along the path she had trodden the previous evening, and then started descending to the beach. Triffy was amazed at the huge difference between the cliff face as she had seen it the day before and as it appeared now. It was no longer the frightening overgrown jungle in which she had lost her way. The paths were well defined and clear of vegetation, and every available level piece of land jutting out from the cliff was planted with vegetables and flowers and a few fruit trees. These irregular cultivated patches were divided by ridges of chalky rock or fissures, and some were surrounded by rough palings to keep out hens and wildlife. But furze, bramble, ivy, thorn, hazel, elder and clematis constantly threatened to invade the gardens, for in the warm wet climate, plants of any kind could shoot up overnight like magic.

Instead of chalets hidden behind high hedges there were sheds made out of driftwood, with roofs of felt or sacking covered with black tar. In these were stored tools, sacks and panniers. There were also linhays, some of them rather ramshackle, where donkeys and poultry were housed. The only parts of the cliff face which remained completely untamed were the deep chasms and hollows between the plats, which were full of bushes and trees. Another spring gushed out towards the bottom of the path.

'Why grow vegetables on a steep cliff?' asked Triffy.

'Because it's sheltered and warm. We never have a frost, so the teddies are ready to dig up long before the ones grown in Branscombe. Later on you'll feel how hot the sun can be here, even in May.'

'It's a crazy place to have a garden.'

'It is hard work. The soil isn't deep and it has to be fertilised with manure and seaweed.'

'Seaweed!'

'Seaweed keeps the soil moist. In the autumn I go down to the sea every day to scrape seaweed off the rocks with a special hook. I hate that job most of all.'

'Why don't you just pick it up off the beach?'

'Because it often gets oily and then it isn't any use. The worst task is digging the seaweed into the soil. Davey does that with manure my father fetches from Humps Farm.'

'Where's that?'

'Up the cliff and across the fields. Walter Broomhill at Humps Farm owns all these plats. He rents them out to people who don't earn enough to keep their families or who don't have vegetable gardens of their own.'

Triffy was puzzled to see no sign of life on the other plats. 'Are you the only people who live here?' she asked.

'Yes, just us and an old man called Amos who lives at the bottom of the cliff in a shed. The other farmers live in the village and come out here when they've time. Davey decided to make the linhay into his home years ago. He's too surly and violent a man to work for anyone. At that time, my parents lived in a cottage in Branscombe. My mum died and my dad lost his job as groom-gardener at Brake House.'

'Why did he lose it?'

'He developed TB and was told not to do heavy work.'

'What's TB?'

'Tuberculosis. It's a disease of the lungs. Dad isn't strong enough to do jobs like chopping wood, scything grass, hedging and ditching, or shearing or harvesting. So he was thankful when Davey asked him to share the linhay and help with the lighter work on the plats.'

'How old were you then?'

'Eight and I'm eleven now.'

'How could you bear to live here all that time?'

'It's better than nothing. It's a roof over our heads and food and a warm place in winter.'

'But not having a bathroom must be awful!'

'We didn't have a bathroom in our cottage. I'm used to fetching water from the spring. In warm weather I can wash at the spring or go for a swim.'

'At the children's home we had three bathrooms and three toilets.'

'Only rich people have bathrooms round here.'

So far, what little Triffy had learnt of life in Davey's linhay didn't appeal at all. She considered her own life in Sidmouth had been dreary and lacking in many of the comforts young girls enjoyed in well off families; but compared to living in a rough hut with no amenities and a slave-driver uncle, it seemed quite tolerable.

Phena was so sure-footed, she fairly skipped down the steep incline, but Triffy often stumbled in her effort to keep up. Just above the beach was a shed with an upturned boat serving as a roof. Alongside it were rows of blue-green cabbages, onions, carrots and a bed of parsley.

'That plot is called Eli's Ground,' said Phena. 'He's lucky to have a plat down here so he doesn't have to lug his seaweed up the cliff. And he can bring provisions by boat from Beer or Branscombe.'

On reaching the beach, Phena took Triffy westwards along the shingle and pointed up at the cliff face. 'Look, you can see many of the plats from here. That shed with the withy crab pots standing by the door, is called Donkey Plat. To the right is Sandy Ground. To the left of Donkey Plat is Tom Selway's plat, and Nellie's Ground. Then comes Edgar's Ground, where another path comes down to the beach. Up there, just below Donkey Linhay Rocks, is Piles Hollow, and further over Neddy Purse's House. Higher up you can just see New Plot.'

'Are there vegetable gardens on other cliffs?' asked Triffy.

'Maybe, if there's been a landslide. Over a hundred years ago the land slipped on this cliff, and when the earth and rocks had settled, there were all these ledges.'

'The land won't slip again, will it?' enquired Triffy nervously.

'No, it's probably slipped all it's going to for a good while yet.'

Phena took the basket off her back and stood it on the pebbles. 'We must hurry now. Help me fill it with driftwood.'

This was no easy task. There was wood enough but it was spread far along the shore and some of it had to be broken up to fit in the basket.

'The weather's getting warm now, so we'll soon let the stove out,' said Phena.

'How do you cook without the stove?'

'On a small kerosene burner.'

'Who does the cooking?'

'I do of course. The men wouldn't demean themselves.'

'What do you cook?'

'Mostly vegetable stew, sometimes with a bit of chicken or bacon or rabbit in it. Edgar gives us mackerel, and we have eggs from our hens.'

'Don't you ever buy fish and chips or beefburgers or pizza?'

'I've never heard of those. We have fish with boiled potatoes.'

'How dull. Don't you have anything sweet?'

'Oh yes, fruit, and Nellie gives us honey. And my aunt in Branscombe makes jam roly-poly and apple pie. We mustn't talk any more, or I'll be late.'

Triffy picked up a few more pieces of kindling, but then the long-necked cormorants perched on top of small isolated rocks attracted her attention. She watched closely as the nearest one, with its metallic blue and green plumage and its weird staring green eye, waddled comically to the edge of the rock and dived in. These birds looked just like the ones she had seen on Sidmouth beach, and it was strange to think that those birds must be the descendants of the ones she could see here. Great banks of seaweed clung to rocks on either side of the beach and in the distance, as the bay swept round in a wide curve, she could make out four massive headlands. Somewhere along the coast must be Sidmouth.

When Phena had filled the basket she observed amiably, 'You're not much help, are you? I suppose you've never gathered firewood before.'

'No, if people want to light fires they buy logs.'

'Davey just chops down a tree.'

Triffy helped lift and strap the basket onto Phena's back and they started up the cliff. The sun was rising as they staggered along, the older girl weighed down and the younger still weary from the exertions of the previous day. They passed a spring from which they drank. Phena said it was their nearest source of water, and several times a day they all had to come and fill their cans. Back at the linhay, Davey and Jack were outside sorting teddies. Phena was instructed to make three journeys that day to Sweetcombe Farm, just beyond Weston, taking altogether, one hundred and twelve pounds of the new potatoes. Triffy was horrified. Three journeys! What kind of existence did this poor girl have to endure?

She followed Phena into the linhay and watched her place four cold cooked potatoes and a bag of barley into a large kerchief. 'Is that all you're going to take to eat?' asked Triffy.

'Yes, my uncle keeps a close eye on the food.'

'Well, I'm starving already.'

'You had my porridge. That should be enough till midday.'

Triffy felt a twinge of guilt, but she said sulkily, 'I don't want to walk all the way to Weston.'

'You could come on one journey, surely.'

'Okay, just one journey.'

CHAPTER 7

In the pleasant warmth of the sun, Triffy watched the white donkey being loaded. Topsy was an emaciated, sad-looking creature, who staggered a little under the weight and Triffy wondered how he was going to climb the steep path.

'Topsy isn't well,' Phena told Davey. 'He's still off his food. You should put him out to grass and buy a young donkey.'

'He's good for a few more trips,' replied Davey.

'His feet should have been trimmed two weeks ago.'

'He can wait. The farrier charges more than I can afford.'

'His eyes need bathing. I'll do it before I go.'

'No you won't. Joe'll be waiting. Get along with you!'

Triffy would have told Davey what she thought of his callousness, but Phena said no more. Topsy started along the path with the girls following. With all the vegetation cut back, the stretch of path leading to Eli's Seat was now a smoother walk. In fact, the whole of the well-trodden main path running across the cliff was easier to traverse.

'What a horrible man your uncle is!' stated Triffy.

'Yes,' agreed Phena. 'He expects Dad and me to work seven days a week, but he's given us a roof and a job and we have to obey him.'

'Couldn't your dad find some other job?'

'I told you, there's nothing much he can do,' reiterated Phena. 'He plants and he hoes. He sorts out the vegetables and he helps me fetch water. He makes scarecrows and elder wine.

Jobs like that – nothing too strenuous. We're lucky Davey has helped us out.'

'I don't agree!' broke in Triffy indignantly. 'Your uncle is the lucky one, to get two slaves.'

At the spring where Triffy had first drunk on the plats, they stopped to rinse their faces and arms, and fill their bottles. Then Phena urged the donkey on gently as the path began to climb, until they emerged onto the cliff top. Now there was no signpost to be seen, only a herd of Devon Reds, deep russet-coloured cattle matching the red earth, who backed away a little as the donkey passed.

Phena led the way inland across the large field and turned into a muddy cow track enclosed by high hedges, where a few last primroses and some stray bluebells grew amongst a mass of cow-parsley, stitchwort and red campion. Phena had to lift her skirts to avoid the fresh wet manure, and soon Triffy's trainers were covered with it. As she squelched along spattering her legs, she yelled angrily, 'Why d'you bring me through this stinking stuff? We could have taken the coast path.'

'Because when Topsy's loaded it's easier for him to walk on the level. We'll come back along the coast part of the way.'

'It's too late. My shoes are covered with muck.'

'My shoes are always muddy. They soon dry off. You can wipe them on the grass at the other end.'

'They'll still stink.' Triffy decided she loathed the country. She wished she could go back to the children's home.

The track brought them to a stony lane running past Humps Farm. 'That's where our landlord, Walter Broomhill, lives. He raises the rents on the plats each year. Davey swears he'll murder him one day, and I wouldn't put it past him. All the land from Manor Mill in Branscombe to Sheepwash Vale, belongs to Humps Farm – that's two hundred and sixty-five acres.'

Triffy glanced at the gaunt grey farmhouse with its tall casement windows and its front yard strewn with muddy gravel and rusting bits of farm implements. There was no flower garden to relieve the dreary prospect round the house.

Two female faces appeared at an open window upstairs.

'Who are those girls?' asked Triffy.

'Pam and Sally Broomhill. They're twins.'

'They're watching us.' But then Triffy remembered that she herself couldn't be watched. It occurred to her suddenly that being invisible might be fun, for a while at least. She could enter forbidden places and do more or less what she liked. She could be a poltergeist and scare people. She could pinch food. A ghost could have definite advantages.

One of the farm girls poked her head out of the window and shouted, 'Talking to yourself again, Triphena? It's the first sign of madness. You'll be locked up in the loony bin.'

Phena walked on without a word, and Triffy despised her for not retaliating to the sharp-faced farm girl. 'I'd have given her a mouthful,' said Triffy, 'if she could have heard me. Why didn't you stick up for yourself?'

'It's no use,' said Phena, 'Pam's father might turn us off our plat if I row with her.'

They continued along a straight lane beside the trotting donkey. 'Are all the roads round here just covered with mud and stones?' asked Triffy in surprise.

'Of course. What else would they be covered with?'

'Our roads are covered with tarmac, which makes them smooth and hard and much easier to walk on. I hate walking on stones,' grumbled Triffy.

'We're nearly at Weston,' said Phena, 'and then it's just a short way to Sweetcombe Farm.'

Phena stopped to examine the spring flowers in the hedge, which were a study in shades of blue. 'I found some viper's bugloss in this hedge last year.'

'Do you know the names of all these flowers?' asked Triffy.

'Yes. My mother taught me, and before she died she gave me her book on wild flowers. I've looked for the more uncommon plants ever since.'

40

'Wild flowers are pretty,' conceded Triffy, 'but who cares what they're called?'

'Town people don't usually care to learn the names of flowers or trees or birds.'

'So what? Why should they?'

A few moments later they reached Sweetcombe Farm and Phena led Topsy into a courtyard where a man wearing a well-worn leather coat and a leather cap was waiting with a horse and cart.

'Morning, Phena. Not like you to be ten minutes late.'

'Topsy isn't well,' replied Phena.

'That uncle of yours should pension him off. 'Tis wicked, making him work in that condition.'

'I've told him, but he won't listen.'

Triffy looked on as Phena and Joe transferred the teddies with the earth still clinging to their gleaming white skins, into a sack which he heaved onto the cart. When Joe had moved off towards Sidmouth, Phena led Topsy to a drinking trough. Then the girls returned along the lane to the village and took the path down through woodland on the eastern side of Weston Combe. The beech trees were in new leaf, a delicate fretwork of luminous apple green against the pale blue sky. Beneath the trees, a shimmering lake of white ramsons and bluebells spread as far as they could see.

'Isn't it beautiful!' exclaimed Phena. And even Triffy was so impressed she fell silent.

Topsy, who knew his way home, presently turned off onto a narrow grassy path running level along the side of the valley until it emerged into the open and began to ascend gently to the cliff head. They travelled slowly to allow the donkey to nibble the prickly stemmed plants. Triffy realised they would eventually reach the same cliff head where she had rested on her way to the plats. Down in the valley she could see the route she had taken on the further side of the stream. Now there was no fence running along the opposite side of the gully carrying the stream, and the ravine was choked to the top with thorn bushes and small trees. There was still a stile at the top of the cliff path. At that time, she had been too hot and exhausted to take in the view, but now in the clarity of a fine May morning, she was exhilarated by the scene.

The sun was shining on a long sweeping curve of salmon-pink cliffs, topped with lush green vegetation all the way round the bay. On this occasion, Triffy noticed with interest how the upper slabs of two sections of these cliffs were ornamented with sculptured rock formations. The towering land mass dropped almost vertically into a light blue sea splashed with patches of dark turquoise. Frothy white wavelets moved in slow, soundless motion against the pristine white shingle. Several upturned boats lay on the beach, and a flock of black-backed gulls skimmed past at eye level.

'You can just see the eastern end of Sidmouth beach,' said Phena. 'The rest of it is hidden behind that nearest headland.'

'Do you ever walk along the coast to Sidmouth from here?' asked Triffy.

'Yes, but it's dangerous to take Topsy. I go by road and then across the fields.'

'On my way here yesterday,' went on Triffy, 'I walked down to that beach, down hundreds of steps.'

'I've never seen any steps. What would you need steps for?' For once Triffy had no ready answer to give.

'This is where I saw you asleep on the grass,' said Phena.

'I did hear someone laughing and a donkey braying.'

'I only saw you for a moment, but then you disappeared, so I knew you were a ghost.'

'I'm not a ghost,' protested Triffy yet again.

'Well, what are you?'

Triffy was baffled. 'Maybe I'm a ghost now, but I certainly wasn't when I sat down here yesterday.'

'What does it matter?' said Phena. 'You're here now and we can be friends.'

'Who says I want to be your friend? I'll go back to my own life tonight.'

'Maybe.'

They moved on along the edge of the cliff. Now, in addition to the hedge of thorn bushes, there was an abundance of tall pungent plants with dark glossy leaves and yellow flowers.

'My mother used to cut the stems of those alexanders to make soup,' said Phena. 'They taste like celery.'

'I hate celery.'

'Have you ever tasted it in soup?'

'No, and I don't want to.'

'I'd like to make soup with alexanders, but Davey won't eat anything wild, not even mushrooms.'

'I hate mushrooms too.'

'You'd eat them if you were really hungry.'

They continued walking beside two fields carpeted with an assortment of wild flowers. Phena told Topsy to wait, and then squeezed through the fence into the second field.

'We can sit here and eat our potatoes.'

'I hate cold potatoes,' said Triffy, but she was the first to finish her share, and secretly enjoyed them.

'Shall I tell you the names of all these flowers?' suggested Phena.

'I won't remember any of them.'

'Yes you will, one or two at least. Over there, garlic mustard, and the lilac one is the cuckoo flower.'

'I don't care.'

But Phena was not to be put off. 'You must know what those are,' she said, pointing to a great mass of plants at one end of the field, each consisting of a circle of wrinkled toothed leaves from which sprang a tall stem bearing many yellow drooping flowerets.

'No I don't!' snapped Triffy.

'You've never heard of cowslips?'

'I may have heard the name. Why d'you go on about these stupid flowers? Garden flowers are much prettier.' She noticed a huge, single scarlet poppy at the edge of the field, and plucked it angrily.

'You shouldn't pick poppies. Their petals only last a few hours.'

Triffy recalled the notice she'd seen about the preservation of wild flowers. 'Seeing as you're so clever, I suppose you've seen a blue gromwell?' she said grumpily.

Phena stared at Triffy in amazement. 'I thought you didn't know any of the wild flowers.'

'I don't. I just saw a notice saying the blue gromwell is a very rare flower.'

'It is – very rare. I may be the only person in Branscombe who's seen one. It's my secret.'

'Why should it be a secret?'

'Because I don't want anyone to dig it up.'

'So what if they do?' Triffy was beginning to wish that, having found herself in the year 1912, she could at least have met a girl who was more like herself, not this peculiar half-grown-up person, who worked all day and went on about flowers.

But Phena wasn't ruffled by Triffy's offhand tone. 'Sometime I might show you where the blue gromwell grows.'

'I'm not bothered.'

Instead of the stile Triffy had climbed over on her journey to Branscombe, there was now a gate leading to the shallow valley which Phena said was known as Sheepwash Vale. Here the grass was covered with dark brown pellets.

'What are those?' asked Triffy.

'Sheep droppings, of course,' laughed Phena.

'How should I know? I don't go on country walks. There's nothing much to see.'

'You could spend the rest of your life walking these cliffs, and there'd be something interesting to see every day. Don't you know the name of any plant?'

'I know a daisy and a dandelion.'

Phena giggled and Triffy flushed with annoyance. 'I don't care about anything in the country!' she shouted.

'No one says you have to care,' Phena pointed out patiently. 'If you'd been brought up in Branscombe you'd know without realising it, just like you know about the sun and the moon.'

Triffy walked on in sulky silence for a while until Phena asked, 'Do you go to school?'

'Yes, but I often play truant. I hate school.'

'I went to the village school until my mum died, then Davey said I didn't need more education to work on the plats.'

'Aren't you lucky. Everyone has to go to school in my life.'

'I'd love to go back and learn more. I can read and write and do simple arithmetic, but that's all.'

'Do you work on the plats in the winter?'

'There's not so much to do in the winter. I spend three days a week at my aunt's house making lace to sell, but it's very slow work. At weekends I sometimes help out as a kitchen maid at Brake House.'

'Don't you ever have a day off?'

'No. Davey doesn't go to church. That's why we have to work on Sunday. Tell me about your life.'

Triffy said bitterly, 'My dad put me in a children's home when my mum died. There's nothing more to tell.'

'What do you do there?'

'We have to help with cleaning and washing up and gardening. But I get out of it whenever I can.'

'What do you want to do when you grow up?'

'Earn lots of money and live in a big house with a swimming pool. I want to watch videos and go to shopping malls and discos and pop concerts, whenever I like. I want to wear the latest gear and eat beefburgers and chips and pizzas and ice cream.'

'I don't understand all those words.'

'Don't you want to be rich and have a good time?'

'I don't know. I've never thought about it.'

Triffy was puzzled. Surely everybody wanted to be rich?

The sun was climbing higher in the cloudless sky as they walked briskly over the spring turf to the beginning of the plats. At the little gate, they met a man on his way up carrying a drum of kerosene strapped to his back.

'Been to Weston already, have you, Phena?'

'Yes, Eddie.'

'Davey drives you hard, don't 'e?'

'Yes, Eddie.'

The man smiled and moved on. Some of the cliff farmers had arrived and were hard at work on their plats, hoeing and harvesting. A couple of them were engaged in clearing a large patch of brambles. 'That's a hard job,' said Phena. 'It takes up so much time, but it must be done almost every day in the spring and summer. Everything grows so quickly.' When they reached the linhay, they found the door shut with a wooden bar which fitted into iron staples on each side.

'The men are out,' said Phena, 'so we can go in and talk.' Inside they drank water and shared a hunk of bread.

'I could do with a Mars bar!' said Triffy. She was astonished to hear that Phena had never tasted a sweet or a chocolate. What kind of a dreary life did this poor girl lead?

'At Brake House where I work,' said Phena, 'the family eat chocolates out of a big box tied with a red ribbon, but the servants are never offered any. Sometimes we have leftover cake in the kitchen.'

Soon it was time to make the second trip to Weston. While Phena was loading teddies into the panniers, Triffy decided to accompany her friend after all. She had no desire to go, but there was nothing else to do. To avoid the mucky track to Humps Farm, they varied their route by walking along the coast and then taking a straight path inland to the Weston road. By this time, Triffy felt a blister developing on her heel. 'My foot's hurting and I wish I hadn't come,' she complained.

Phena promised to put some herbal ointment on it when they returned. 'You should wear stockings like I do.'

'Children don't wear stockings in my life. D'you wear those ugly boots and stockings all the year round?'

'Yes. I haven't any other shoes. When my boots wear out, the village cobbler makes me another pair.'

'Don't girls ever wear sandals?'

'Not in Branscombe. Everyone needs strong shoes for walking.'

'In my life people don't walk everywhere. They use cars or motorbikes or buses.'

'We have steam lorries to deliver coal and grain. Most people use a cart or a wagon. A few men own bicycles, but walking is the only way on the cliffs.'

'If I were you, I'd refuse to make three trips a day to Weston.'

'I'm used to it. Davey can't shout at me and I can look for wild flowers. In good weather I enjoy it.'

'Does your uncle pay you?'

'No. He says children shouldn't get a wage. Keeping me in food and clothing is all I should expect.'

Triffy couldn't understand how Phena put up with such hardship. At least at the children's home there had been some treats to relieve the monotony, and every evening she'd watched television for an hour. 'Do you even work on Christmas day?' she asked Phena.

'No, we go to my aunt's for dinner. She keeps ducks and we take sprouts and turnips. It's the best day of the year because Davey never comes. He sits in the linhay and gets drunk.'

By the time the girls had completed the round trip again, it was past midday. Davey and Jack were eating potatoes and onion soup in the kitchen. They had left a portion in the pot for Phena and it was agony for Triffy to watch her consuming it. If she was going to remain in this life for more than a day or two, hunger would be a problem. She moved into the bedroom and noticed a large, dilapidated old book on a shelf, entitled *Classification of Flowering Plants*, by A D Smith. On the flyleaf was written the name, Alice Fielding, and below it, Triphena Edgecombe. The drawings in colour were old-fashioned, thought Triffy, and the descriptions were hard to understand. Words like generic, perennial and lanceolate made no sense, and she decided botany would be a dull subject to study.

In a while, Phena brought her a piece of bread spread with rancid beef dripping, and a tin mug of milk. 'It's all I dared to take,' she said, 'but this evening, when the men go out, I'll make you some porridge. There's plenty of oats in the sack.'

'I can't eat porridge without sugar,' stated Triffy crossly.

'It's porridge or nothing, I'm afraid. Here's some ointment to rub on your foot.'

CHAPTER 8

Phena went outside to load the donkey for the last trip, but when she saw Topsy looking so weak and miserable, she went in and told her uncle he needed a good bran mash and a night's rest.

'He can do one more journey,' growled Davey.

Phena appealed to her father. 'You always used to say, Dad, that we should treat animals kindly. So are we going to let poor Topsy go on suffering?' Jack looked shamefaced, but dared not oppose his brother. Triffy longed to say what she thought of them.

'I'll not take Topsy again today,' announced Phena firmly.'

'Refuse to work for me, my girl, and you can clear out. Go and live with your aunt.'

'You know I'll not leave Dad.'

'Off you go to Weston then.'

Triffy felt outraged at the thought of another trip for the poor donkey, and she was still desperately hungry, so when Phena and the men left the linhay, she stayed behind to search for food. In the cupboard she found the end of a loaf, a piece of cheese, and best of all, two large pasties. She stuffed them into her rucksack and for the first time since arriving on the plats, she felt quite cheerful. She and Phena deserved this food for all the effort they were expending, and Davey wouldn't be able to accuse Phena of stealing, as she hadn't been alone in the kitchen since returning from Weston. How useful it was, being invisible!

Phena nodded to her and they set off. When they were out of earshot, Phena said kindly, 'Don't come if your foot's hurting.'

'Of course I'll come,' retorted Triffy in her contrary way.

It was distressing to see Topsy struggling along so patiently with his burden, often stumbling on a stone. Triffy had never observed an animal closely before and she was put out to see how pathetic a sick creature could look. Phena kept patting him and encouraging him with gentle words. 'Topsy is the only donkey on the plats who isn't treated well. I feel so ashamed of his condition.'

'What will Davey do tomorrow if Topsy can't walk?'

'I expect he'll buy another donkey on the cheap and work him to death too.'

Taking his time, Topsy managed to reach Sweetcombe Farm. Then, as the girls sat on a log to rest, Triffy produced the filched provisions triumphantly from her rucksack. Phena was disapproving at first, but she was as hungry as Triffy and soon ceased to care what her uncle would think. They stuffed themselves in utter contentment. Triffy judged it the best meal she had ever eaten. She had never known hunger in her own life, and it was almost worth starving for a while, she thought, in order to savour even dry bread.

They allowed Topsy to dawdle as much as he liked on the way home and it was after five when they reached the linhay. Davey, having discovered that all the food was missing from the cupboard, was in a rage. ''Tis not the first time Ben Trim's robbed me. He had my broad beans last summer.'

Phena and Triffy followed Davey down the path and listened to him berating his neighbour. A row ensued, and several of the cliff farmers gathered to defend Ben. In the end, Davey retired to fume inside the linhay.

'See the trouble we've caused,' Phena whispered to Triffy.

'Too bad. I can't help it if your uncle is so mean.'

Triffy sat on the stool in the corner watching Davey's hard little eyes darting about suspiciously. She hated the way he shovelled stew into his large mouth, letting the gravy run down his beard. After the meal, Phena took down the hurricane lamp from the roof beam and trimmed the wick before lighting it. Without a word, Davey and Jack went out on their nightly visit to the inn, and at last the girls were able to talk.

'I'll make porridge for you now, and enough for your breakfast too. We can hide it in the bedroom,' said Phena. Cold porridge would have revolted Triffy the day before, but now any food was better than nothing. And as Phena pointed out, they were going to need plenty of sustenance the next day on their way to Sidmouth to take bunches of anemones to the market. Triffy was about to say she wouldn't go, when she suddenly realised it might be interesting to see what Sidmouth had looked like in 1912. And being invisible meant she could go into shops and pick up whatever she wanted in the way of food. It might even be fun to wander into the children's home and spy on everyone. Yet that might be too risky. What if she were whisked back to 1994 while she was there?

Phena usually made one trip a week to Sidmouth during the late spring and early summer. In addition to these journeys with Topsy, she had to undertake various other tasks. The weekly washing had to be delivered to her aunt's house in Branscombe. Bread and meat had to be bought. She had to look after the needs of the donkey and the goat, to clean the hen house and to carry water from the spring.

'Dad helps me when he isn't feeling too weak.'

'In my life,' said Triffy, 'children aren't allowed to work unless it's just a small job, like delivering newspapers. And they get paid for it.'

Triffy had spent only one day sharing Phena's hard life, but she felt as though she had been living on the plats for a week. She'd always rather despised children who did as they were told, but she couldn't help admiring the way Phena coped with the endless round of tasks. And strangely, the older girl's patience made Triffy feel less resentful against her own lot.

At six in the morning, they set out on the long walk to Sidmouth. Topsy was carrying panniers of anemones glittering with dew which Jack had tied in bunches the previous evening and left to soak in metal buckets. Triffy was surprised that the donkey was still able to walk, but his sad expression made her want to give Davey some hard kicks.

Beyond Sweetcombe Farm, Phena took a short cut across fields and then they walked down a track to the village of Salcombe Regis. Topsy surprised Phena by passing a garden without attempting to nibble some early rosebuds hanging over the hedge.

'He must be very sick. Rosebuds are his favourite food.'

By the time they reached Salcombe Hill leading down into Sidmouth, they were already tired, and unlike the previous lovely clear day, the sky was overcast, and a bitter east wind made walking unpleasant. It was sure to rain before the day was out.

How odd, Triffy thought, to be returning to Sidmouth without ever having reached Branscombe. On the journey she had been planning what she might pinch in the town. Her rucksack was much too small and she wished she could fill the panniers with provisions. And why stop at food? She could take anything she liked. What fun to play fairy godmother to her friend. But how would Phena hide such things? It was most frustrating. As they neared the bottom of the hill, Triffy put her idea to Phena.

The older girl was horrified. 'You can't turn into a thief just because you're invisible! I wouldn't touch stolen food.'

'It's different, being a ghost,' protested Triffy. 'Surely a ghost can do what it likes. I won't pinch much, just some food and a few clothes.'

'No, you mustn't!'

'Well I can't go on wearing these clothes for ever. What will I do when my shorts wear out?' But Phena wouldn't change her mind. Shoplifting was wicked.

At first, Triffy thought the town looked much the same as she had left it. Elegant white houses with wrought iron balconies, trellis porches, tent-shaped canopies and shady lawns, were still in evidence. But there were no telephone wires or TV aerials, and all the modern buildings had disappeared. So had the cars and lorries and vans. Instead there were hansom cabs and old-fashioned bicycles and pony traps.

Triffy observed that the smarter women were wearing plain long skirts and striped cotton blouses under velveteen coats, with hats, gloves and silk bags hanging on chains from their wrists. All wore black stockings with dark boots. Some of the better-dressed men were wearing knickerbocker suits and belted Norfolk jackets with matching narrow-brimmed check hats. Others wore three-piece tweed suits and turn-up trousers over black woollen socks. Collars were worn high up under clean-shaven chins, and footwear was made in black patent leather. The poorer men looked shabby in collarless shirts, shapeless trousers and dusty boots. In a dress shop, several outfits in the window were priced in guineas. Triffy had heard the word before, but had no idea of its value.

In spite of the sound of dogs barking, carts clattering down the cobbled streets, bicycle bells and people gossiping, the town seemed very strange and quiet to Triffy.

They turned down a narrow lane which Triffy knew well, and Topsy was tethered in a small courtyard. Two women were busy sorting flowers into mixed posies of white, purple, crimson, blue and shades of pink. They were working against time and barely looked up when Phena unloaded her anemones. But they said, 'Bye bye, see you again next week,' as she led Topsy away.

They retraced their steps, with Triffy keeping behind Phena in the crowded narrow street. As they passed a bakery full of customers, Triffy couldn't resist snatching up two large currant buns, one of which she consumed before they reached the river. They sat on the grass under a tree to rest, and Phena fed Topsy some oats. Then Triffy announced, 'I've got you a bun, Phena.'

'You've stolen it!'

'Yes, I have,' retorted Triffy angrily. 'I'm starving. I'm sick of porridge and potatoes and dry bread. I'm going to run back to the shops and pick up a few more things to eat.'

Without waiting for an answer, Triffy raced along Salcombe Road and back into the High Street. She enjoyed herself immensely, snatching up fruit and cake and cheese and a pork pie until her rucksack was full to bursting. She half expected Phena to have gone, but she was still sitting on the grass persuading Topsy to eat.

'I'll not touch anything stolen.'

Triffy was infuriated. 'I can't sit here eating these nice things in front of you.'

'Go on, eat them. You're a ghost, so maybe it's different for you.'

'Actually, I'm not a ghost,' persisted Triffy annoyingly. 'If I was a real ghost, I wouldn't need anything to eat.' She gobbled down half the pork pie, hating Phena at this moment.

'I don't understand what you are,' said Phena sadly. 'I don't want you to disappear, and I don't want you to be hungry. So you must do as you like. But it's wrong to steal.'

★

Later, as they were trudging up the steep thickly-wooded hill, they failed to notice the weather was changing for the worse, until they reached the summit and saw the bank of angry black cloud hanging over the valley.

'We're going to get wet,' said Phena as they heard a distant rumble of thunder. 'But we can't hurry poor Topsy.' The sick donkey was exhausted long before the rain began to fall in a heavy curtain of water as they were leaving Weston. On the path from the road to the coast, he had to be coaxed along inch by inch, staggering all the way. He seemed to revive a little on the grassy path, until there came a razor-sharp zigzag of lightning which ripped the clouds apart, followed by several gargantuan claps of thunder.

Topsy's legs gave way under the monstrous impact of sound, and he collapsed onto the turf at the edge of the cliff. All Phena's gentle persuasion failed to make him rise. The sky had turned an eerie shade of yellow. The sea seethed under a steely-grey surface and the whole cliff seemed to be in motion. Then a wind raced along the beach, dashing the swollen sea in a frenzy against the land. Gulls were tossed this way and that in the cold air, and the few stunted trees on the cliff edge, were flattened.

Triffy had memories of thunderstorms in Sidmouth, when she had been fascinated by the noise, but glad to be safely indoors. But it had been nothing compared to being exposed high up on Weston Cliff with the wide, raging sky bearing down on them. Alone, she would have been paralysed with fear, and collapsed like the poor donkey. But with Phena, she knew hardship had to be faced.

The girls were forced to the sodden ground, their faces and hair streaming with water. Phena knelt over the spent animal, begging him not to die. But it was no use. Topsy's overworked frame had had enough, and a few moments later, Phena was burying her face in the dead donkey's wet fur, sobbing her heart out. This was a different Phena from the calm, mature girl Triffy had seen so far. Triffy herself, who had never had occasion to feel sympathy for anyone in extreme distress, was now moved to tears. Impulsively, she placed her arm round Phena's thin shoulders.

The wind dropped a little and eventually they rose and with difficulty, unstrapped the panniers from Topsy's back. Phena looked around and then plucked some dripping yellow alexanders' heads and some white sea campion and laid them carefully over the donkey. Then she picked up the panniers and continued along the path with Triffy at her heels. It was not until they began to descend into Sheepwash Vale that they were able to walk side by side. Triffy offered to carry the heavy panniers for the rest of the journey.

CHAPTER 9

The storm had passed over and a sudden shaft of sunlight broke through the banks of sullen grey cloud, casting a copper sheen over the dark sea. They rested for a while on the wet grass, their clothes clinging damply to their chilled bodies.

'Your uncle will blame you,' said Triffy.

'Of course he will. He'll swear at me all the more for knowing it's his own fault. He could afford another donkey. My aunt says he's plenty of money put away.' She paused, and then said bitterly, 'He's a wicked man, I hate him! But what can I do?'

Triffy was boiling over with rage against Davey. *If I'd been Phena,* she thought extravagantly, *I'd have pushed him over the cliff by now, or poisoned him.*

By the time they reached Eli's Seat, the sun was shining, and Triffy sank onto the damp wood saying she wanted to dry off.

'Come when you're ready,' said Phena. Triffy's mouth was full of cake when she saw Davey come storming up the path from the linhay, followed by his brother. Instinctively she leapt off the seat and flattened herself against the rock, but she needn't have moved for they were quite unaware of her. She returned hurriedly to the linhay and found Phena cutting up vegetables.

'What did your uncle say?'

'He wasn't as angry as I thought he'd be. He just cursed Topsy for not making it back here. They've gone to push the body over the cliff.'

'Is he allowed to do that?'

'I don't expect so, but Davey's too mean to hire a horse and cart and take Topsy to the knacker's yard.'

'What's a knacker?'

'A man who disposes of dead horses and donkeys.'

'Is he going to buy another donkey?'

'I can't take our produce to Weston if he doesn't. Tomorrow I have to take the washing to my aunt's, so we'll manage without a donkey for one day.'

Triffy was relieved. 'That's great. I want to see Branscombe, if I'm still here.'

★

When the men returned for supper, Triffy, who had rested for an hour on her bed, ate the remaining food she'd pinched, and then went out to explore the plats. In the aftermath of the storm the evening light had taken on a luminous quality, casting a soft pinkish-yellow glow over the vegetable gardens. This made the assortment of sheds and bits of fencing and netting mixed up with piles of driftwood, and logs, sacks, flowerpots and patches of scrub, appear less untidy than they looked when she had first seen them.

She walked past Eli's Seat, intending to find the spring in the bamboo copse. Phena had told her there was a spring just below some large ivy-covered rocks. Triffy found it, but there was no bamboo, or indeed any cultivated flowers round the spring, so she returned to the main path leading downhill. Halfway down she stopped to listen to a couple who were feeding their donkey a bran mash before settling it for the night.

'I saw Phena come home without Topsy. I reckon the poor creature's dead,' said the man.

'Pity Davey don't drop dead!' replied the woman. 'Jack should take Phena out of his clutches afore she goes the same way as the donkey. Alice would turn in her grave if she knew what was happening to her daughter. That girl was bright at school. She should be getting an education.

'All these years on the plats without companions of her own age have turned her into such an odd little thing. She's not like a child at all.

'The village children laugh at her ragged clothes and her shy ways. They call her a witch. 'Tis a shame, for she's a good girl.

'It's partly on account of her mother, they call her a witch. Alice Edgecombe could see things the rest of us couldn't.'

Davey and Jack had gone when Triffy returned to the linhay. Phena gave her some stew, and then they went outside to wash the bowls in a bucket of water. Both girls were so tired they could hardly stand up, so they went straight to bed. They were woken up when the men came in drunk and clattered their way round the kitchen. Then Triffy told Phena what she had overheard.

'Why do the kids call you a witch?'

'When I sing or talk to myself, they spy on me and say I must be talking to the devil. It doesn't matter what they think. It's all nonsense anyway. But I've always wanted a friend to take my part.'

'I'm a bit like you,' confided Triffy. 'Actually, I think it would be fun to be a witch and cast spells on people I don't like. But now I'm a ghost, I can think of ways to frighten people who are nasty to you, especially Davey.'

Phena sat up in agitation. 'No, you mustn't. People might say it was me casting evil spells. They'd say I was possessed by the devil, and lock me up.'

'But if I frightened Davey when you weren't there, how could he connect it with you?'

'Please leave my uncle alone. He has such a terrible temper, he could do anything if he's annoyed. Up to now I've been lucky. He's only beaten me once, when he was very drunk.'

Triffy's eyes widened in horror. 'If I see Davey hitting you I'll kill him!' she threatened with furious bravado. 'I could use my catapult to aim stones at him.'

'You must promise not to do anything like that. I would get the blame.'

'Why should you get the blame? It would be an accident.'

Phena leapt out of bed and leant over Triffy. 'You must promise!'

'Okay, okay, I won't kill him.'

Phena smiled and returned to her bed. Triffy drifted off to sleep, half hoping she would be back in 1994 by the morning, and half hoping to remain in 1912.

CHAPTER 10

At half past five in the morning, Triffy heard Phena get up and make breakfast for the men. When they had gone, the girls shared the rest of the pan of porridge. Then Phena stuffed the washing into her basket and they set off to Branscombe. Phena led Triffy over a stile and then up a very steep, new path which emerged onto a wide grassy track with a good view of the bay far below. This was the path Triffy should have taken off the plats on the night she arrived, had she not been drawn by the sound of music towards Davey's linhay.

They passed a number of large grassy humps sparkling with early morning dew, then turned inland and picked their way eastwards along a rutted cart track full of puddles. Through the trees, Triffy caught glimpses of the village down in a valley.

'There are many paths to Branscombe,' said Phena. 'We'll take the one leading to the church.'

They plunged through the woods, and after slithering down a sloping wet field, they crossed a footbridge over a streamlet and climbed a stile into the churchyard. Here, ancient yew trees with fluted trunks, spread their branches over heavy crosses on ugly black plinths, and stone table tombs weathered into shades of white, rust, mustard and green. The church itself, a tiny grey square-towered building lying peacefully in the early sunshine, blended perfectly into the green valley.

'Do your family go to this church?' asked Triffy.

'No, my aunt goes to the Wesleyan chapel. Mostly it's the gentry and their servants who use this church.'

'What's gentry?'

'Upper class folk like the family I work for at Brake House.'

Triffy had never been inclined to enter a house of worship, but this little church attracted her. 'Can we go in?'

'Of course,' replied Phena. 'Anyone can look in.'

They walked past two stone pots full of tulips perched on either side of the little stone porch and pushed open the heavy nail-studded door. On their left, stood a large stone font elaborately decorated with floral carving. 'What's that for?' asked Triffy.

'It's a font. The priest puts water in it and baptises babies. It was brought here last year from East Teignmouth when they did the alterations to the inside of the church.' Phena pointed to the rows of pews smelling strongly of new wood and varnish. 'These pews were put in to replace the old box pews made of cheap deal.'

'What's deal?'

'Planks made of fir or pine.'

Triffy looked up the long narrow aisle with its honey-coloured walls and shining flagstones, to the chancel arch, beyond which lay a stone and wood screen guarding the tiny sanctuary. Feeling the antiquity and peace of the church, Triffy was silent for a moment. This place was a far cry from the hall at school where the children sang hymns each week sitting on bright orange, plastic chairs.

'What's that wooden thing up there?' asked Triffy.

'That's the pulpit where the priest stands to give a sermon.'

'How do you know all this if you don't go to church?'

'My mother used to bring me to see the church when it was empty. She liked sitting here quietly. So I come sometimes by myself.'

'It's a nice place, but I don't like the musty smell.'

'The damp makes it smell. I don't mind it. We must hurry now,' and she led the way out of the church.

They turned up a roughly cobbled road running through a long, vivid green valley where horses were grazing on the juicy spring grass. Eventually they reached a few cottages where the road forked uphill on either side of the village inn. Phena said the left-hand fork led to Humps Farm and the right-hand to her Aunt Dulcie's cottage. This was a cream-washed house of cob and thatch with a large garden and an apple orchard. At the front were haphazard beds of aromatic wallflowers, forget-me-nots, jonquils, sweet williams, lavender and pinks. Starlings perched in a row on a shed. Beside the extensive vegetable plot at the back, stood a small wash house of galvanised iron.

Inside, Dulcie and her eldest daughter, Primrose, had already started their own household wash. Phena suggested that Triffy stay outside and watch through the window, since it was hot and damp inside, with very little room – even for a ghost! Triffy rested her chin on the window sill, but could see nothing at first owing to the clouds of smoke and steam. There was an overpowering smell of warm wet washing.

When she was able to make out the scene inside the wash house, she was amazed. Instead of the usual gleaming white machine into which laundry was thrown, there was a huge copper, perched over a flat square, brick fireplace. Beside it stood a rectangular wooden wash tub resting on a long wooden form, in which the clothes were being scrubbed with soap, soda and laundry blue, before being dropped into boiling water.

On the opposite side of the room stood a mangle with a tin bath beneath it to catch the drips. On another form, stood a second tin bath into which the wrung clothes and household linen were laid prior to being placed in a wicker basket ready to be pegged onto wire lines in the back garden.

Dulcie was a small but robust woman, encased in a stiff white apron and a mob cap, her face flushed with exertion and her hands swollen and red with scrubbing. Primrose, a girl in her teens, was a younger version of her mother. She emerged from the wash house with Phena and together they operated the windlass to draw up two more buckets of water from a well. Later Phena came out with a basket of clean washing.

'You can help me,' she whispered. 'I don't expect they'll notice.' The washing lines were held high off the ground by poles which had to be lowered. Since the girls were quite short, it was hard work pegging on the sheets and towels and preventing them from trailing on the plants while they hoisted up the pole again. On another line they hung out calico chemises, flowered muslin smocks, nighties, lace petticoats and drawers. Some of the clothes were made of such thick, heavy material that Triffy wondered how they ever dried.

'We'll walk down to the bakery before we peg out my washing,' said Phena. This idea sounded more interesting to Triffy than washing. They retraced their steps to the church, passing a horse-drawn bread van full of fresh loaves. Triffy was overcome by the delicious smell and could hardly wait to reach the thatched bakery, a short way down the hill from the church, opposite a forge. Dough for the second baking was proving in two enormous wooden troughs, while the baker bagged up plain flour from the nearby mill with baking powder, to sell. He had put by a few loaves from the early morning baking for customers like Phena, who came to collect their bread. The baker's wife, in white apron and cap, was making little cakes, tarts, buns and scones to be baked in a small oven built into the large fireplace.

While Phena was making her purchases, Triffy helped herself to one of the loaves from the first baking, and began to tear pieces off and cram them into her mouth. It was such bliss, she determined to come here again and help herself to whatever she wanted. If only Phena's uncle had owned the bakery instead of a vegetable garden!

Phena had noticed Triffy eating. 'If you go on stealing we can't be friends any longer,' she said miserably.

'I shall go on pinching food and I don't care if we're not friends. I hope to wake up tomorrow in my own life, but if I'm still here, I'm not going to starve.'

'Starve! You eat as much food as I do and I'm not starving. You don't know what it means to be really hungry.'

'Oh yes I do,' returned Triffy, 'I've been really hungry for three days.'

'You're just greedy.'

Phena bought an ounce of tobacco at the village shop and then they returned to Cotthayne Cottage in silence. Sulkily, Triffy helped Phena hang out another load of washing. But Phena could never be cross for long, and she said, 'I always have a cup of tea with my aunt. Do you want to come in and see her house?'

'I suppose so,' answered Triffy. 'There's nothing else to do.'

They entered a large cosy stone-flagged room where a massive oak dresser decked with blue and white crockery filled one wall opposite an equally large beamed fireplace. Three tabby cats sprawled over a well-worn handmade rug in orange and brown stripes. Dulcie and Primrose were seated at a scrubbed wooden table, drinking tea poured from a plump earthenware pot. They had removed their mob caps to reveal smooth dark hair parted in the middle. Phena joined them while Triffy went to look at a glass-fronted cabinet full of examples of fine lacework, labelled in brass frames. She noted two of the peculiar names – Honiton Sprigs and Branscombe Point.

'Just wait till I see that brother of mine!' Dulcie complained to Phena. 'Davey's trousers are the filthiest things I have to wash by a long way. Black with grime and stiff with salt. He ought to change them more often. He could afford a few more pairs of trousers. I've a good mind to make him pay for my work. And it's high time he paid you a wage, Phena, so you can buy yourself some new clothes. You look a right scarecrow in our hand-me-downs. I'd like to see you in a pretty white frock sprigged with pink roses. A cuckoo in the nest was our Davey, and no mistake. Jack should have learnt to steer clear of him.'

'I know, Aunt Dulcie, but what else could he have done?'

'He should have taken you to Sidmouth or Exeter and found himself an office job. It'd be better than being a slave to Davey. But there, it's none of your doing. You're a good girl, and if I didn't have four daughters to raise all on my own, I'd give you a home here.' Then she added, 'They've lost the chambermaid up at Brake House. Wouldn't you like a permanent place there? You'd get fed well and some of your clothes provided, with a soft bed and time off, and best of all, a good wage.'

'It's good of you to think of me, Aunt Dulcie. If I left the plats, Davey would make Dad leave too. It's hard on the plats, but there's the trees and the flowers and the birds to look at. And the sea. At Brake House I'd be indoors all day.'

'Well, I shall tell Davey he must give you time off to make friends of your own age in the village. You're alone too much.'

'I've nothing in common with the village children. They don't want me.'

'You're a strange girl, Phena, very like your poor mother, and too much strangeness will do you no good in the end.'

When Phena had drunk her mug of tea, Dulcie said, 'Here, take this pasty and a couple of jam tarts. But don't you share them with Davey. And there's a jar of crab apple jelly.'

While Phena was putting the clean washing into her basket in the garden, her aunt hurried out, saying, 'Before you go, I want to take a photograph of you. The girls gave me a box Brownie camera for my birthday. Go and sit yourself on the front wall.' Phena ran to the wall and arranged herself on it, while Triffy slipped out of the gate. She crept up behind her friend and put her arms round her waist just as Dulcie took the photograph.

'When will I be able to see it?' asked Phena excitedly. 'Not for a few weeks. I don't want to finish the film too quickly.'

CHAPTER 11

As they left the village by a path leading up from the inn, Triffy asked, 'Did you make some of the lace in your aunt's cabinet?'

'Yes.'

'How do you make it?'

'If it was winter, I'd show you. You make it using bobbins on a pillow, or you can make a cheaper lace using a needle.'

'Could I make it?'

Phena smiled. 'You'd be too impatient.'

'Why don't you demand a wage from Davey? He wouldn't get anyone else to work for nothing.'

'I know he'd refuse. Dulcie thinks he might be saving every penny to emigrate. Then I'd have to go into service, and Dad would be left with no home.'

'Don't you wish your aunt had been able to bring you up?'

'Dulcie is very kind, but she's bossy and never stops talking. I like to be alone sometimes. Sitting on Eli's Seat by myself at sunset looking at the sea is what I enjoy best. At Cotthayne everyone is always shouting or laughing too loudly or teasing.'

Triffy was puzzled. She hated being alone for long. She liked noise and activity going on all the time.

Phena was used to carrying the heavy basket of washing up the hill. Halfway Triffy offered to take it, but by the time they reached the top she was panting with the effort. 'You're not very strong, are you?' observed Phena. 'What makes you so weak?' Triffy flushed with humiliation, though Phena had not meant to be disparaging.

'I'm not used to walking up and down hills all day. I hate walking, and I hate Branscombe. It's a dead boring place. I like towns best.'

'We have everything we need here. We have a builder, a blacksmith, a butcher, a cobbler, a carpenter and a baker. There's a post office, a cider press, a mill and a grocery. We even have a packman who calls with cloth and haberdashery.'

'Not the kind of shops I like,' insisted Triffy, sullenly.

This time they entered the plats through another small wrought iron gate. 'What are these little gates for?' asked Triffy.

'To keep out the cattle.'

Triffy glanced up and saw a great boulder of rock perched dangerously at the edge of the cliff. 'That rock might fall on us.'

'I expect it will one day,' replied Phena cheerfully.

Back at the linhay, the girls had lunch, sharing the pasty and the jam tarts, sitting on the grass outside in the sunshine. Triffy wanted to lie on the grass all afternoon, chatting, but Phena had more work to do. The washing had to be hung out to finish drying, wood had to be gathered and vegetables prepared for supper.

To add to the tasks, Davey appeared with a basket of anemones and said Phena must make another trip to Weston with the flowers.

'Why can't I take them tomorrow?'

'Because there's a few teds to carry in the morning.'

'Aren't you going to buy another donkey?'

'Maybe, when I can afford it. In the meantime we mustn't waste our produce. Hurry now, and tie those flowers into bunches.'

He left the girls on their own, and immediately Triffy shouted furiously, 'I'm not walking to Weston again! I hate your uncle. You should refuse to go. You're too weak to stand up for yourself.'

'If you come with me,' persuaded Phena, 'we could go down to the beach and have a swim on the way home.'

'It's much too cold to swim in May.'

'The water's cold, but the beach is sheltered. You soon get warm in the sun.'

'I bet it's absolutely freezing.'

'Who's a weakling now? I've swum on a sunny day in January.'

'You're just a show-off!' exclaimed Triffy, but she knew it wasn't so. Phena was simply stating the truth.

'Well, stay behind if you want to,' said Phena. 'Will you help me tie up these flowers?'

Triffy was very slow at this job and only managed to tie six bunches to Phena's sixteen. When Phena set off with the basket strapped to her back, Triffy said nothing, but she followed. Perhaps children in her own life *were* rather feeble. She had begun to have a sneaking admiration for the more hardy children of the past.

Without the donkey, Phena could spend more time looking at plants as they crossed the field. She picked two slender, four-petalled yellow flowers and held them out to Triffy. 'They look the same, don't they? But they're not. This one with the bigger leaves and beaded pods, is charlock, and this is wild turnip, with long smooth pods.'

Triffy considered them to be very nondescript plants. 'Are the pods those long thin things below the flowers?'

'Yes, they contain the seeds. Open one and you'll see.'

Triffy opened the charlock pod and saw two rows of five dark reddish-brown seeds. 'They're just weeds,' said Phena, 'but when you look closely, suddenly they become interesting.'

'I don't think so. They're just ugly weeds.'

★

In spite of herself, Triffy enjoyed walking along the coast in the afternoon sunshine, watching the buzzards soaring overhead. After the anemones had been delivered to Sweetcombe Farm, they scampered along the valley path and started down Weston Cliff. Triffy found it no easy task without steps. It was a question of sliding on her behind over the steepest sections. But it was no trouble to Phena. She was like a mountain goat.

The well-trodden path descended westwards, until roughly halfway down it did a hairpin bend to the east. At the bend an ill-defined and even more perilous path led off into hawthorn bushes and a patch of tall, pale green spurge plants.

'We'll go along this path,' said Phena, 'and I'll show you my beautiful blue gromwell.' They worked their way round the hawthorn bushes and found themselves on a narrow overhanging ledge of rock with a dangerous drop below it. Phena moved nimbly along the ledge, but Triffy hesitated.

'It's not safe,' she said.

'Yes it is. Just don't look down.'

Determined not to be outdone, Triffy edged, inch by inch, along the ledge. Then they stumbled over a stretch of thorny scrub and finally reached a rectangular flat stone just wide enough for them both to huddle side by side on their stomachs.

Tucked away in a hollow below this stone, grew a single clump of gromwells. 'Look, there they are!' said Phena. Triffy wasn't much impressed by the clusters of little flowers, each with five petals fused into a slender tube. Some were a reddish-purple and some a brilliant blue, at the top of thin stems with narrow, dark green leaves.

'The flowers aren't all blue.'

'They will all turn blue,' Phena assured her.

'How did you know they were here?'

'Before she died, my mum told me she had once seen a blue gromwell on this cliff. For two years I kept looking until last spring, I found it. It's my secret, and now it's your secret. Don't pick it, or ever tell anyone where to find it.'

'How can I tell anyone if no one can see me?' said Triffy impatiently.

'Just as well, you can't be tempted. A botanist could offer you a lot of money to show him this plant.'

'Just for a silly flower?'

'Oh yes. People who study and then write books about rare plants will pay a great deal to find their habitat – that means the place where they grow.'

'If a botanist offered me money, I'd certainly tell him. I'd be crazy not to.'

'You don't understand. He would dig up this flower and try to plant it in his garden, or he would press it in a book. Then there'd be no more gromwells on this coast. If the clump is left alone it will spread and maybe one day you'll see blue gromwells all over the cliff. Until then, it must be kept a secret.' Triffy was rather flattered that Phena had considered her worthy of sharing the secret, but she still thought it was a fuss about nothing.

'We'll go down and swim now,' said Phena, and she led the way back to the main path. Triffy followed, feeling slightly dizzy. She didn't want to walk along that dangerous ledge again, yet later, when she looked up from the beach and saw the section of cliff they had crossed, she felt quite proud of having done it. There was no one in sight on the beach and it was certainly very warm. So Triffy took off her grubby shorts and tee shirt and soaked them in the stream running over the shingle. Then she spread them over some gorse bushes to dry. It was a wonderful feeling to be rid of clothes that had become uncomfortably dirty.

Phena took off her skirt and blouse and thick worsted stockings and garters. Triffy stared at Phena's very white body standing in calico drawers, and doubled up with laughter. 'What funny knickers!'

Phena in her turn was astonished at the sight of Triffy's tiny scarlet briefs. 'Do all children wear clothes like that in your life?'

'Yes. Only old ladies wear thick stockings and knickers and high necks.'

'What do you wear in the winter?'

'Trousers and jumpers and socks.'

'Don't you ever wear a skirt or a dress?'

'I don't, but some children do.'

'I'd die of shame if I had to go out in your clothes.'

'So would I in yours,' retorted Triffy and they both giggled.

In spite of the sunshine, the girls hadn't bargained for the iciness of the spring sea. Phena struck out strongly against the current and Triffy did her best, but neither could bear the cold for long. They resembled two shivering corpses as they dripped over the shingle with no towels to wrap themselves in. Then Triffy shouted, 'Bet I can beat you to that boat,' and she sprinted away, hoping to find herself better at something than Phena. To her disappointment, she and Phena touched the upturned rowing boat at exactly the same moment. But for once she had shown herself equal to Phena.

'Let's run back to keep warm,' suggested Phena, and they raced along the edge of the surf till they reached the extensive spread of rock at the western end of the beach. Phena's feet were hardened to clambering over the prickly surface, but Triffy could only move slowly in bare feet. They squatted down to gaze into the limpid pools among these rocks, stained with hues of red and green and smelling of salt and iodine. The deeper pools were filled with the swaying, branching feathery fronds of brown seaweed.

'Look at the tiny, tiny crabs,' said Phena. Triffy had never examined a rock pool. Why, she wondered, hadn't she ever explored the rock pools at Sidmouth?

Triffy's clothes had dried enough to put on, and she was dressed in a moment. Phena took longer to put on her stockings and button up her blouse.

'Don't you wish you had a tee shirt?'

'It would be quicker to dress, but I'd feel queer in that shirt.'

Triffy was helping to strap the flower basket onto Phena's back, when suddenly a small pebble hurtled through the air and struck her on the side of the head. A second pebble caught her on the shoulder. The girls looked up and saw four boys standing near the top of the cliff path. A third pebble sent Phena running for protection under a stone wall surrounding a coastguard hut, while the boys laughed and whistled.

'Who are those boys?' asked Triffy.

'They come from Beer, just along the coast. Pete Derryman is the ringleader. His father is a fisherman who used to work a plat. He and Davey had a row and Pete's father was evicted. Davey took over his plat, and in revenge, Pete and one of his friends came over from Beer and pinched Davey's strawberries. The second time Davey caught them at it he gave them a thrashing. Ever since then, Pete has taken it out on me.'

'Why don't you tell Pete that you hate Davey as much as he does?' asked Triffy.

'Because those boys never come near enough to talk to.'

Soon the boys moved on and the girls were able to start up the east coast path. Triffy noticed that the deep ravine on their left didn't look the same as when she had first climbed up this path. Then, the steep sides had been cleared of vegetation, but now the whole ravine was filled with small trees, thorny bushes and a mass of thick undergrowth. The stream bed could no longer be seen. Surprisingly, Triffy found her leg muscles had become stronger and she was able to climb the arduous route without feeling too fatigued.

CHAPTER 12

When they reached the plats, Phena began to look for suitable pieces of firewood amongst the scrub. Triffy found it frustrating that now they were within earshot of the cliff farmers, they had to stop talking. But she cheered up when they found Davey had left a note on the table saying he and Jack wouldn't be back for supper.

Phena produced a hunk of bacon with some bread and spring onions, hoping to satisfy Triffy's appetite, but Triffy refused to touch the bacon. 'Yuk! I hate fat. We never had bacon like this at the children's home.'

Phena was indignant. 'That's how bacon comes from the pig. If people only ate the lean part, most of the pig would be wasted.'

'Well, you can eat it. It makes me sick to look at it!'

Phena cut herself a thick slice and then found a small stale lump of cheese for Triffy.

'Don't you ever have butter?' Triffy demanded petulantly. 'Or even marge?'

'What's marge?'

'You don't know anything, do you! It's yellow stuff you spread on bread.'

Tomorrow, thought Triffy, *I hope I'll be gone. But if I'm still here, I'm going to pinch some more food.* 'Where do you buy butter?' she asked.

'At one of the farms.'

'And jam?'

'Everybody makes their own jam. I'd make it, but Davey's too mean to buy the sugar.' Then Phena became suspicious. 'Triffy, you're not to steal butter or jam. If Davey found any here, he'd thrash me.'

'Your dad should protect you.'

'Davey's too strong for my dad.'

'How do you put up with it? I can't stand being here much longer!'

Phena regarded Triffy with a sad smile. 'It's not such a terrible life when you have a friend. But I know you can't stay here for ever.'

Suddenly, Triffy felt guilty. She was beginning to like this strange old-fashioned girl. There was something rock-solid about Phena in spite of her small frame and gentle ways. She'd never let you down. Triffy felt she didn't really deserve to be liked by such a person.

'Promise not to steal from my aunt,' said Phena. 'She can't afford to lose her food.'

'What about the rich people?'

'You don't know where they live.'

'I'll soon find out.'

'Can't you see the trouble it would make for someone? An innocent person would be suspected and punished for your theft.'

'I'd be very careful to take only what wouldn't be noticed.'

'My aunt would know if a crumb of cheese was taken.'

'I won't pinch anything from her, of course.'

After supper, Phena took the washing off the line and then settled down to darning her father's thick woollen socks.

'You must be mad, mending socks!' exclaimed Triffy. 'You can buy a pair for 50p at the market.'

'How much is that?'

'I think it used to be called ten shillings.'

'Ten shillings for socks! Who could afford that? Why don't you darn your socks?'

'No one darns socks!'

Phena was darning her father's grey socks with bright blue wool which, she explained, was some of her aunt's leftover knitting wool. 'In any case,' said Phena, 'Davey will never buy new clothes if the old ones can be mended. Haven't you ever learnt to sew?'

Triffy admitted she had once sewn on a button, but it had fallen off the next day.

'What can you do that's useful?' asked Phena seriously.

'Nothing. I hate work.'

★

The following day, Phena was instructed to take as many vegetables as she could carry to Weston. Triffy had had enough of traipsing to Weston. Now she knew the way to Branscombe, she would go and explore the village at her leisure. 'See you later,' she said and hurried away before Phena could reply.

She climbed up to the humps and taking the path leading down to the church, she wondered which way now – up the valley, or down to Branscombe beach? It was going to be fun entering any house she fancied. She decided to walk up to the inn and then on to Humps Farm. It would be interesting to visit the Broomhill family, especially the girl who had taunted Phena. And if there was any food to pinch, it would serve them right.

She walked past rows of whitewashed and stone cottages with smoking chimneys. Behind hedges of privet and elder, beech and hazel, lay vegetable plots surrounded with strips of spring flowers. Out of low stone walls grew masses of red and pink valerian and yellow wallflowers. In every garden, vegetables held pride of place; flowers were an afterthought, and for the most part, grew higgledy-piggledy. There was no planting in neat rows as in the Sidmouth gardens.

Presently, after trudging up a steep hill, Triffy recognised Humps Farm on her right. In the front yard, a dozing collie leapt up barking, his fur standing on end. But no one appeared.

Triffy approached the front door, turned the handle and opened it·inch by inch until she could see into a long dark hallway. The floor was covered with mud-stained green linoleum and the white walls were hung with stuffed foxes' heads, a stuffed pheasant, a stuffed duck and a gun rack. An enormous mahogany hatstand, out of which peered a stained and yellowing mirror, dominated one wall. Opposite leaned an eight-day grandfather clock with a single hour hand.

A door was open to her right and Triffy walked into what felt like a very unlived-in front parlour, smelling of dried lavender. Two ungainly horsehair armchairs and a sofa positioned on a Turkey carpet, took up most of the room. Brass candlesticks and photographs and samples of lace in brass frames were ranged across the top of an elaborately carved sideboard. *Lace again,* thought Triffy. *Everyone makes lace.* A rag doll with corn-coloured wool hair was perched on the mantelpiece under a faded picture of King George and Queen Mary. In one corner stood a silver-gilt cake stand, and in another corner, a treadle sewing machine. The plum-coloured velvet curtains were partially drawn across the two windows, giving the room a gloomy air.

Triffy took down the rag doll. The button eyes in its grubby face stared up at her without expression. On a small table lay a circular chocolate box, which Triffy opened guiltily. To her disappointment, it contained only buttons and pieces of ribbon. She put it down and slipped out of the room.

Now she could hear voices behind a door at the end of the hallway. For the first time she attempted to go through a door without opening it, and found herself in a large square kitchen with a single black beam across the ceiling. A delicious smell of roasting meat and pastry filled the air. Triffy half expected the three people in the room to jump up at her entry, but they appeared to have no inkling of her presence. Two red-cheeked girls, obviously twins, with brown hair parted in the middle and tied back with blue ribbon, were seated whispering and giggling to each other on a high-backed settle tossed about with cushions covered in bright hexagonal patchwork. As she watched them shelling broad beans into a colander, she thought, *These must be the girls who shouted at Phena through the window.* A big-boned, strong-looking woman stood in front of the cooking range, stirring something in a copper pot.

'Hurry up with those beans, you girls. Your grandmother will be here any minute, and there's still the strawberries to see to.'

This was the most interesting room Triffy had ever been in. The smells, the textures, the shapes and the colours, all combined to stimulate her senses. And being invisible, she was able to let her eyes wander across the room and back, dwelling on each object as long as she wished. There was too much to take in all at once, but certain objects caught her attention – a giant copper kettle suspended on a crook on one side of the open hearth, and a gleaming preserving pan on the other. A blue and white check cloth spread on a solid elm table. A row of pewter mugs dangling from nails in a huge dresser on which were displayed floral bowls and plates and serving dishes. A basket of green duck eggs, a square of newly baked gingerbread and four crusty loaves standing on a pine worktable. Strings of golden onions and dried bunches of sage, thyme and rosemary hanging from the beam. Freshly washed cotton garments airing on a rack above the fire. Wrinkled apples lying on shelves in a dark recess together with terracotta jugs of elderflower wine. Two earthenware pots of cream on the table on either side of a vase of blue irises. A tin bath leaning against the wall next to a brass candle snuffer. A hefty marmalade cat curled up on a scarlet mat on the stone-flagged floor...

She would have noted many more things if one of the girls hadn't left the kitchen by another door and then returned carrying a tiny newborn lamb in her arms. She sat on a stool and proceeded to feed it from a bottle. Fascinated by the sight, Triffy moved close to the lamb and ran her finger gently across its woolly head. It stopped sucking and jerked away from the bottle, letting out a plaintive 'baa'. Then it resumed its feed. Triffy backed away, not daring to touch it again.

She was about to snatch up a loaf from the table, when she heard the noise of a pony and trap clattering across the cobbled backyard.

'That'll be your grandmother,' declared Mrs Broomhill as she hurried out of the room. Triffy followed, passing through a back kitchen where small jars of pickles and huge jars of cider were kept on shelves. A large white bowl piled high with glistening early strawberries stood on a marble-topped stand. Coats, sou'westers, knives and a billhook hung on the walls, and boots littered the uneven floor. Triffy opened her rucksack and emptied half the strawberries into it.

Out in the yard, an old lady in a black dress and a black bonnet was being helped down from the trap by a young man in a smart tweed suit and cap. The pony suddenly whinnied loudly and champed at his bit. One of the twins offered him an apple and he calmed down, crunching up the fruit with his thick yellow teeth. Triffy wished she could have given him something to eat.

The old lady swished past Triffy in a stiffly lined, black silk dress with a high bosom, her stays creaking as she went. They all followed her into the kitchen where she sat down in a Windsor chair. After exchanging a few pleasantries the grandmother said, 'That plats girl, Triphena Edgecombe, walked past my house this morning, laden with vegetables like a donkey! Jack should know better than to let that slip of a girl carry so much.'

'Sally and I think she's mazed, Gran. We see her going up the lane to Weston talking as though she had someone with her.'

'No wonder if she's mazed, the life she leads. That uncle of hers should be horsewhipped.'

'She scares us,' continued Pam. 'We go down to the plats sometimes and she stares at us in such a peculiar way and never speaks. You should see her clothes, the state they're in. I don't suppose she ever takes a bath, living in that old linhay.'

'What do you go down to the plats for?'

'To pick sloes and crab apples and hazelnuts. The cliff farmers yell at us to go away, but why shouldn't we pick the wild fruits? It's all Dad's land, isn't it?'

'Keep away from the plats,' said the grandmother sternly. 'It may be your dad's land, but he's rented it out to the cliff farmers, who have to work very hard to earn a living. They don't want you hanging about.'

'Why doesn't her dad live in a proper house in the village?' asked Sally.

'Because he's a sick man and can't afford the rent. Triphena's mother, Alice, was a well-educated woman with very refined ways. It was a sad day for the little girl when she died and Jack lost his job and his cottage. Since then he's been under the thumb of his brother. Triphena's a good girl, so leave off annoying her.'

'Yes, Gran,' chanted the twins, but Triffy knew they didn't mean it. In revenge she picked up the gingerbread and fled into the hallway and out of the house.

★

She went back to the church and then continued down the village street. Dense overhanging woods of larch and beech, oak and sycamore, rose high above her as she followed the curves of the long sinuous valley to the sea. A sudden tidal wave of sheep swept down one of the steep fields below the tree line. Then they dispersed, leaving soft wisps of cream wool hanging over the hedge. Further down the valley half a dozen young heifers scampered along the fence, aware of her presence though unable to see her.

Triffy stopped when she saw the bakery, situated behind a long white cottage built on the hill. Opposite, two horses stood patiently outside the thatched smithy while their riders chatted to the blacksmith just inside the entrance. On one side of the smithy, alongside a large field, ran one of the many Branscombe streams. Something about the scene seemed familiar. She had seen this smithy before, when it had been next to a large modern building with a clock above the door. She and her father had stood outside this long white cottage. This was where her grandmother lived, only at that time the house had been pink. The longer she considered, the more she was sure her memory was correct. She had reached the very house she had set out from Sidmouth to find, but now it was no use. In 1912 her grandmother hadn't yet been born. If she knocked on the door, a complete stranger would answer. It was a weird and frightening thought. If only she could be transported to 1994 right now!

She stood for a long time hoping for her wish to come true, but nothing happened. So she walked on down the curving village street until she lost sight of the sea in the midst of another group of cottages and a thatched inn. She found a track running beside the stream which she guessed would take her in the right direction, and soon enough she found herself at Branscombe Mouth, on a long stretch of shingle. There was no sign of habitation on the deserted beach apart from one solitary building, a culm house in which, Triffy later discovered, coal dust was stored to fuel the lime kilns on the coast.

She strolled along the beach and sat down on the pebbles to eat the stolen strawberries. They tasted delicious, and soon her hands and face were stained pink. Sitting alone by the sea, Triffy wondered what was going to happen to her. With Phena, she felt like an ordinary person, but now the thought of being a ghost for ever, unable to communicate with other human beings, was terrifying. Being invisible could only be fun for a while. Phena would grow up, but surely a ghost couldn't grow up. A ghost couldn't die. What was a ghost?

CHAPTER 13

Triffy watched a flock of herring gulls taking flight from the water, crying 'kyow, kyow' as they went. Several landed near her, so she was able to observe them closely for the first time – their grey backs and their grey wings with black tips and white patches, their large yellow bills with a red spot and their flesh-coloured legs. She had seen them so often at Sidmouth when they were scavenging for food on the esplanade. Till now, birds had just been creatures which flew or settled on branches. She had never cared to examine one closely, nor had she realised there were so many different kinds, all with individual habits.

Suddenly she wondered if she would be able to find Phena again. She must get back to Davey's linhay quickly. She could see a path winding up the western side of Branscombe Mouth across a sloping field and disappearing into woodland. She would risk taking this route, rather than trudging all the way back along the village street. She crossed over a stile and continued walking through woodland until she came to the series of grassy humps which would eventually peter out at the entry to the plats. It must be well past midday, judging by the sun. Phena should be home by now. She began to run in her anxiety to see someone she could talk to again.

The door was open and Phena was sitting, utterly worn out, on a bench. But she smiled in delight when she saw Triffy. 'I'm so glad you've come. I thought you might have disappeared into your own life. Davey and Dad have gone to see someone at Beer. They won't be home till late.'

'I enjoyed being a ghost today,' said Triffy.

'Where did you go?'

'To Humps Farm. I saw those horrible twins. They were saying nasty things about you.'

'I don't care.'

'Are you hungry?' asked Triffy, pulling the gingerbread out of her rucksack.

'Did you steal it from Humps Farm?'

'Of course I did. They deserve to lose it. They've got so much food in that house, it won't make any difference to them.' Triffy grinned and added, 'You don't have to share it. You can just watch me eating it.' She broke off a piece and took a large mouthful. 'Come on, have some.'

Phena's willpower gave way and in a few minutes, the girls had finished all the gingerbread.

'My gromwells have turned bright blue. Would you like to see them?' asked Phena.

'It's such a dangerous path.'

'But if you fell, you wouldn't come to any harm, would you, being a ghost?'

'I don't want to.'

'All right. Tomorrow is Sunday and I won't be going to Weston. After I've finished my jobs we could go to Branscombe Mouth and walk along the landslip path to the Hooken Rocks.'

'Okay.'

★

When they had cleared the table they walked to Eli's Seat. It was the stillest of evenings, warm and balmy, with the promise of a good summer. A mother-of-pearl sea lay immobile beneath an opalescent sky, over which were spread fingers of the palest apricot, crossed horizontally with fine bands of wispy cloud. In the hazy distance the range of cliffs looked mauve, with veins of ochre. Once again Triffy was intrigued by the variety of colours and shapes in the sky and landscape. In Sidmouth, if someone had asked her to describe the sky she would have said that it was blue when sunny, and grey when cloudy.

'Guess who I met today,' said Phena.

'Who?'

'A botanist called Mr Bond.'

'What was he doing?'

'Looking for a blue gromwell! He offered me fifty guineas if I would show him where it grows.'

'Did you show him?'

'Of course not!'

'Think of all the things you could buy. The botanist will probably find it on his own.'

'No, he won't. He's short and fat, and it will be hard for him to get down the cliff.'

'Did you tell him you'd seen a gromwell?'

'Yes, but I said I wouldn't show him where it was.'

'How silly of you. You should have said there are no gromwells on the cliff.'

Now that the blue gromwell had proved to be so valuable, Triffy was beginning to feel as keen and protective an interest in the flower as Phena. If only she herself could deter Mr Bond from exploring the cliff. Perhaps she could use her catapult to good effect. She would have to think about it.

As the days became warmer, so the flowers round Eli's Seat – brilliant orange and yellow bird's foot trefoil, green spurge, early purple orchids, pink thrift, yellow rock roses – were spreading in profusion. Phena was able to tell her the name of every plant in sight.

'When I fell asleep here on the grass I saw some tiny flowers. One was white and purple with a yellow spot, and another was blue.'

'Eyebright and milkwort,' said Phena.

'You're so clever!' said Triffy sarcastically. 'Are there any flowers you don't know?'

'There are hundreds I don't know. But I hope I know all the ones on this coast.'

'You could be a botanist.'

'I'd have to go to school and take exams. You have to know everything about plants, not just their names. What would you like to be when you grow up?'

Triffy had no idea, but she said quickly, 'A pop star. That's someone who sings with a group and earns lots of money.'

'D'you mean a folk singer?'

'No, not a folk singer. If only you had a radio we could listen to some pop music.'

'What's a radio?'

'It's a small box-like thing. You press a button and you can hear music, or the news, whatever you want to hear.'

'I haven't heard much music. The Salvation Army band plays in the village sometimes. I like to listen to that, and my aunt sings hymns and folk songs at Christmas.'

'We sing hymns at school. I hate them.'

'It's not real work is it, singing with a band?' ventured Phena.

Triffy was indignant. 'Of course it's real work. A pop star has to spend hours learning songs and how to sing them. They earn fabulous salaries, especially when they sell their discs. And don't ask me to explain a disc. It's just a round plastic... no, just a round, shiny flat thing you put into a machine and it plays music for about an hour.'

This idea was beyond Phena's wildest imagination. 'Have you got a music machine?' she asked in wonder.

'No, of course not. It's only for rich people. I haven't even got a radio of my own.'

After a pause Phena asked, 'So what will you do when you leave school?'

For once, Triffy replied honestly. 'I don't know. I'll fail my exams, or I won't bother to take them. At sixteen they'll turn me out of the children's home. At least, they will if I'm sent back. But I came here to live with my gran.'

'What's her name?'

'Harriet Garland.'

'I've never heard of anyone called Garland in the village. You're so lucky to be at school. Why don't you work hard, and then you can have an interesting job?'

'I hate school work! I hate any kind of work!' declared Triffy.

'But it's lazy and selfish not to use your brain. Or are you very stupid?'

'No, I'm not stupid!'

'Then you should be grateful for the chance to learn. And at school you can make friends with children your own age.'

'I hate the kids at school!'

'So they hate you back. What good does that do? I suppose you hate me too?'

Triffy was taken aback by this direct question. Then she said vehemently, 'No, I don't hate you at all. No one could hate you – and if anyone tried to hurt you, I'd kill them with my catapult!'

Phena laughed, but she was pleased.

★

As they talked on, relaxed for the first time since Triffy had appeared on the plats, it grew darker. The moon rose, a luminous disc casting a watery ribbon of light across the sea. Suddenly they heard a blood-curdling screech near at hand behind them. Triffy ducked in fright, but Phena caught at her arm, crying, 'Look!' She turned in time to see a white shape floating out of the trees above them, with wide, spread wings; a shape which hovered and then plunged down into the undergrowth.

'A barn owl,' whispered Phena. 'Probably hunting a mouse.'

'It looked like a white ghost. I thought owls were brown.'

'There are different kinds of owl. Barn owls usually live in barns or hollow trees. Sometimes they lay their eggs on a cliff ledge. They never build a nest.'

'How do you know?'

'You get to know about animals and birds and insects when you live in the country. I expect you know things about towns.'

'I don't know much about anything,' said Triffy resentfully. 'The teacher said I was a dumbo.'

'I was put in the dunce's corner once at school because I was watching a spider make its web and not attending to the lesson.'

There came the sound of a long drawn-out, eerie scream which alarmed Triffy again. 'What's that?'

'Only a fox.'

'Will it attack us?'

'Of course not. It would be terrified of us.'

Triffy peered intently at the dark mass of trees beyond the plats, towards Branscombe Mouth. At night, the woods looked much more extensive than by daylight.

'What else lives in those woods?'

'Deer and badgers and lots of smaller creatures.'

'Do you see them?'

'Yes, but you have to sit quietly and be patient. At night you hear things you don't hear during the day.'

'I hate sitting still for too long.' Then Triffy added, 'I saw a reddish-brown deer running up a field at Weston.'

'How did you know it was a deer?'

'I saw a Disney film once about a deer.'

Phena looked uncomprehending and Triffy felt irritated at not being able to explain.

They sat in silence for a while and then Phena said sadly, 'I don't know what will happen to me when I'm older.'

'I expect you'll get married and live in a proper house. I don't know why your dad doesn't apply for a council house. My mum and dad once lived in a council house.'

'There are no houses like that here.'

When the girls got up, Phena cast a shadow across the moonlit turf but there was no shadow where Triffy's should have been. 'Look, you haven't got a shadow,' Phena pointed out. Triffy was most upset. To have no shadow made her feel even more unreal than being invisible. She took Phena's hand for reassurance, but there was no response. Phena couldn't feel it. Triffy's mood changed to one of feeling hopelessly alone. Even the prospects in her real life brought little encouragement.

The girls returned to the linhay and slept soundly, not even waking when the men returned in the small hours.

CHAPTER 14

In the morning they rose early as usual. It was a bright breezy day with little clouds scudding across the sky. Being Sunday, it was very quiet on the plats. Phena led the way past Eli's Seat and the Ivy Hole rocks to the plat Davey rented near the bottom of the cliff, and Triffy followed in great discomfort, for her trainers were wearing out. She would have to pinch some shoes. But where from?

They reached the long thin plat situated just above that belonging to the elderly man who lived on the cliff. 'I must speak to Amos,' whispered Phena. 'He's too old to be a cliff farmer, but he has to keep going to pay the rent.' The bent old man was struggling to hoe his strawberry bed.

'Good morning, Amos,' said Phena. 'How are your strawberries coming along?'

'They'll be ripe in a week or two, but they derches will be at 'em and at my peas. 'Cos they knows when I'm goern in to bed, do they derches. *Amos is goern in to bed*, they sing to each other. Come the autumn I'll have to give up my plat. It'll be the workhouse for me then, me dear.'

'Couldn't you go and live with your son in Australia?'

'No, what would he want with the likes o' me?'

'I wish I could help you, Amos.'

'You've enough troubles wi' that uncle o' yours. Time you left the plats and stopped being his slave.'

While Phena was talking to Amos, Triffy noted how gnarled and red and swollen the old man's hands were, and how bent his shoulders were, how his blue eyes were sunken under the threadbare cap. He must be very old. Yet how beautifully he kept his large plat, planted so neatly with many different kinds of vegetable as well as teddies.

'What's a workhouse?' asked Triffy, when Phena had finished talking to the old man.

'A place where poor people have to go if they have no home and no money. It's like prison, Amos says.'

Triffy had never given a thought as to how old people lived if they were poor. She did recall vaguely hearing about pensioners, but Phena assured her that poor people certainly weren't given any money. The workhouse was the only solution for anyone who couldn't save enough to live on in their old age.

Thrift and valerian and ground ivy had begun to creep in at the edges of Davey's plat, and a variety of green weeds had sprung up among the anemones. Phena gave Triffy a spare hoe and suggested they start at opposite ends. Triffy had never used a hoe, and Phena weeded most of the patch.

'Goodness, you are slow!' said Phena.

'It makes my arm ache,' complained Triffy.

'If you're planning to live in Branscombe, you'll have to learn how to weed.'

'Why will I?'

'Because everyone has a vegetable patch.'

'Stop going on at me. You're worse than a teacher!' snapped Triffy. 'And this place is so hot. I'm going to the spring for a drink.'

Back at the linhay, the girls ate boiled potatoes and peas with bacon dripping, and then Phena prepared vegetables for supper. Triffy helped to wash the dishes in a bucket outside, thinking how much easier it would be if there had been a sink and tap water inside the linhay.

★

Afterwards they took the coast path to Branscombe Mouth and stood on the edge of the highest point of the cliff, looking down over the fishermen's cottages and the culm house. The only sign of life was two men on the shingle, painting an upturned boat. The girls descended and walked a few yards eastwards along the beach. Here, a short section of coast had fallen away in great chunks onto the shore to form a permanent ridge of rocky, almost impenetrable vegetation. They set out on a path leading onto the landslip, from where they could see three massive white pillars of different heights, partly encased in creeping greenery.

'Those are the Hooken columns,' said Phena. Between the cliff and the columns, yawned a wide rocky chasm filled with bushes.

Triffy was entranced. 'Can you climb them?'

'Yes, but it's very difficult. Pete Derryman's brother climbed the shortest column – you can just see it, below the others. But he fell and broke his leg.'

They walked on, and then started up the cliff, and Phena pointed out how deceptive the Hooken columns were. 'From one side it looks as though there are only two columns, but from the top of the cliff you can see there are four quite clearly.'

Suddenly Triffy caught sight of a startling pinpoint of blue in a patch of green below them. For a while she hardly dared hope. But no other flower she had seen had the same sharp distinctive blue. She exclaimed with a delight she had never felt before, 'Look! Isn't that a blue gromwell?' Phena stared down and agreed, yes, it must be a gromwell, the first she'd seen on Hooken Cliff.

The more they stared at the flower, the more it seemed to jump out from its background. 'Mr Bond couldn't miss it, coming down this path,' said Phena anxiously. 'I must go down and dig it up, and then we'll plant it in a secret place.'

'You can't possibly go down there,' said Triffy. 'You'd fall.'

'I'm going to try.'

Inch by inch on her behind, Phena worked her way from the ledge down across a section of scree, until with difficulty, she was able to get a grip on a tussock of grass within reach of the flower. Carefully she dug up the single gromwell plant with her hands and placed it in one of her pockets. Then she climbed back to Triffy, saying, 'How clever of you to see it!'

Triffy experienced her first glow of achievement. 'You'd have seen it soon enough,' she said magnanimously. 'And you dug it up.'

'Well, we saved it together.'

They retraced their steps to the bottom of the chasm, and found a small sunny clearing behind a thicket, where Phena replanted the precious flower.

'We'll come back in a few days and see whether it's taken,' she said, bending over the plant and brushing it lightly with her lips. 'Stay alive, please stay alive!' she whispered.

Triffy noticed a long rent in the back of Phena's skirt where the white of her petticoat now showed through. Her hands and face were grimy and she had lost the black ribbon at the end of her plait. 'I'll have to go to my aunt's to sew up my skirt and get another ribbon.'

By the time the girls reached the beach they both looked like dirty urchins. But it was only Phena who could be seen walking up the village street. People out in their Sunday best looked askance at the girl with dishevelled hair and torn skirt. A group of girls, including Pam and Sally Broomhill, came sniggering behind Phena, saying, 'Where's your broomstick, Triphena Edgecombe?'

When she turned they pretended to run away, shouting, 'Quick, quick, hide, or the witch will put a spell on us!'

Triffy was all for doing something to scare them, but Phena whispered, 'No, it will make it worse.' So they walked on till the girls became tired of bullying.

'You've got to get your own back on those Broomhill girls,' insisted Triffy.

'Perhaps,' replied Phena wearily. She looked very pale and miserable, which made Triffy fume with anger and a desire for revenge.

Further up the village street they encountered a herd of cows, swaying heavily from side to side. Phena moved easily through them, but Triffy hesitated, not sure about walking amongst these huge unfamiliar creatures. When she did advance, they backed away nervously, bumping into each other. Triffy pressed against the hedge until the farmer's boy had urged the cows on.

At last they reached Cotthayne Cottage, where Dulcie was surprised to see her niece in such a state. 'My skirt got torn on a piece of sharp rock,' said Phena vaguely.

'Well, go and get yourself washed while I mend it.'

Triffy followed Phena to the wash house where they cleaned themselves up.

'Here, put this on for now,' said Dulcie when they returned to the kitchen, and she handed Phena one of her own skirts.

'Has Davey told you his plans yet?' asked Dulcie.

'What plans?'

'Davey and your father are emigrating to Canada in a week's time, and they're taking you with them.'

Phena looked stunned. 'Dad's health will never stand up to the journey.'

'Well, you can refuse to go. Take that full-time job at Brake House, and let Jack go to the workhouse until you can afford to keep him elsewhere.'

'Dad will do what Davey tells him. You know what he's like. And if Dad goes to Canada, I must go too.'

'See if you can persuade him not to,' said Dulcie, looking very gloomy.

While listening to this conversation, Triffy became as agitated as Phena. The possibility of remaining by herself as a ghost in Branscombe was appalling. And the situation was made more complicated, when on the way home Phena said,

'If you're still here in a week, will you come with me to Canada? I'm so frightened of going alone.'

Triffy didn't know what to say. She felt that if she went to Canada she might never be able to return to her own life. 'If your dad goes, Phena, that's his own lookout. You should stay here.' But it was no use arguing with Phena.

Jack was alone in the linhay when the girls returned, so Phena was able to speak to him privately. 'Dad, you're not well enough to start a new life in Canada.'

Jack stared at his daughter with a confused, helpless expression on his pinched face. 'Davey has our money and he's already bought the tickets. He wants us to set up house together, and he says you can go to school.'

'He'll not send me to school. It's just a bribe. Why did you allow him to keep all the money we've earned?'

'Because he's the boss, Phena,' said Jack.

'Why not go to the workhouse, just for a while?'

Her father's eyes filled with fear. 'No, Phena, not the workhouse! Anything rather than that!' Tears began to roll down his sunken cheeks.

They heard a bumping noise outside and Davey entered, dragging a large brass-bound trunk. 'I expect your dad's told you we're off to Canada in a week's time. So we've a few days to clear all the vegetables off our plats. We're going to need every penny we can get.'

Phena said bravely, 'Dad and I don't want to come. You give us the money we've earned so we can find somewhere to live here.'

Davey regarded his niece in cold fury. 'Jack and I are sticking together, and you'll do as you're told.'

CHAPTER 15

For the next four days, they hardly saw Davey. He told Phena to make one trip a day to Weston, and Jack to make a bonfire of all the garden rubbish. Triffy remained in a terrible state of indecision, wondering whether she should go with Phena. She felt strongly that she ought to keep near the spot where she had first become a ghost. Phena, who had always been so cheerful and optimistic, had now become downhearted, and even tearful. Triffy accompanied her on the trips to Weston, feeling angry and baffled as to how they were going to cope with the difficulties ahead.

It was nearing the end of May, the time when the countryside was looking its loveliest. Foxgloves were springing up everywhere, and the green tendrils of white bryony were insinuating themselves round the stems of dog roses and honeysuckle.

'At the end of summer this bryony will turn into beautiful necklaces of green, yellow and red berries hanging from the hedges, but I won't be here to see them,' said Phena sadly.

Mr Bond, the botanist, was still staying at Sweetcombe Farm, and Phena worried that he might be hiding to spy on her if she went to look at the gromwells. Before climbing over the stile above Weston beach, they looked around carefully. Triffy found it easier this time to edge her way along the ledge leading to the patch of glittering rare flowers.

'Aren't they the brightest, most lovely blue you've ever seen?' enthused Phena. 'No botanist must be allowed to uproot them.'

'But who's going to guard them when you go to Canada?' asked Triffy. She was becoming as anxious as Phena about the fate of the blue gromwell.

'I wonder if there are wild flowers in Canada?' said Phena.

Triffy recalled seeing a film about Canada. 'I don't know about flowers. There are mountains and lakes and thick snow.'

'If Dad should die on the journey, I'd be left with Davey. You will come with me, won't you?'

'Yes, I'll come, but you know I might disappear at any moment.'

'I know you might.' And Phena said no more on the subject.

★

The week went by until Friday, when they took the last of the teddies to the farm and then went down the west side of the valley intending to swim. They came across Mr Bond puffing up Weston Cliff, his round red face glistening with sweat. He laboured to lift his short stout legs over the high stile and then collapsed onto the grass and lay there, unable to rise.

'Could you give me a hand, my girl? Your cliffs have defeated me.' Reluctantly Phena helped him to his feet. 'I'll find that gromwell in the end, but to save me a lot of trouble I would be obliged if you would tell me where to look. I'm willing to pay you more than fifty guineas for your assistance.'

'Oh no, sir,' said Phena sweetly, 'it's my secret. But I will show you a white corn gromwell.'

'Don't be silly, child. Corn gromwells are extremely common in the fields and nothing much to look at.'

In the meantime Triffy had picked up a discarded gull's feather. She began to tickle the damp folds of fat on Mr Bond's neck. He leapt away in fright and she shrieked with laughter. Phena laughed too as the botanist searched under his shirt for an imaginary insect. When he'd finished heaving himself about, Triffy tickled him again. He turned crimson with rage when he saw Phena giggling at his discomfort. He went stumping off up the valley, shouting that he had never met with such insolence and that the Devon hussy should be horsewhipped.

'Poor man, he looked as though a ghost was after him!' and they continued to laugh all the way home.

In the evening, Davey returned looking like thunder. 'I hear you've just done us out of fifty guineas, Phena – money we could do with in Canada. So you can just go back to Sweetcombe Farm and show Mr Bond that blue gromwell.'

'No, I won't show him, or anyone else.'

'Why not?'

'Because he'll dig it up and take it away.'

'Who the devil cares if he does? One wild flower, more or less, is of no consequence. And it won't matter to you in Canada.'

'I won't show him,' repeated Phena quietly.

At this reply, Davey lost his temper and struck his niece so hard across the face that she fell to the floor, where she lay sobbing. 'And there's more of that to come if you don't do as I say. Get up!' And he kicked her on the thigh.

The moment Davey struck Phena, Triffy looked around for a weapon. She seized the huge, heavy iron frying pan from the range and threw it at him with all her strength, just as he bent to kick Phena. It missed his head by half an inch and smashed against the wall. Davey stared wildly at the pan on the floor, as his brother entered the room. Then he cried in a choking voice, 'My God, Jack, this place is haunted!' and rushed out without another word.

Triffy helped Phena to her feet and then to her room where she lay on the bed for a while holding a cold wet flannel to the livid mark on her face. When she had recovered a little, she returned to the kitchen where her father was sitting at the table with his head in his hands.

'He struck me, Dad, and said he would again if I didn't show Mr Bond the blue gromwell!'

But Jack was too weak in strength and in character to defend her. 'We need the money, Phena. We must do what Davey tells us. He's the one who gave us a home.'

'D'you call this a home, Dad? I'm not coming with you to Canada to be Davey's slave! You'll have to go alone.'

'I'll die if you don't come,' whimpered Jack. 'I need you, Phena.'

Later, when the girls were in bed, Phena whispered, 'Triffy, you mustn't try to help me. If that frying pan had killed Davey, Dad and I would have been blamed for his death.'

'D'you expect me to sit and watch you being attacked?' protested Triffy. 'If only I could push him off the cliff when you weren't around. I must think of a way to scare him into leaving the plats on his own.'

'Davey isn't easy to scare, and there isn't time anyway. We're leaving in two days,' said Phena.

They both lay thinking of the uncertain future. 'Every night,' said Phena, 'I wonder whether you'll be here in the morning.'

'I wonder too,' agreed Triffy. 'Half of me wants to go, and the other half wants to stay here and help you.'

Phena stretched out her arm towards Triffy's bed, saying, 'I want to give you this ring to remember me by, just in case you disappear. It was my mother's wedding ring.'

Triffy took the unusual double band of gold in her hand.

'You can't give me this. It's too precious.'

'I want you to have it, I really do. Then you'll remember me when you look at it.'

Triffy wished she had something valuable to give in return. She opened a little pocket in her rucksack and took out the cheap ring with fake diamonds round a glittery red stone which her father had bought her in Weymouth. 'You can have this if you like. It's not gold like yours.'

'I'd like to have it. It looks pretty on my hand. I'll have to make sure Davey doesn't see it.'

CHAPTER 16

When the girls got up on Saturday morning, Davey had already gone out leaving Jack in bed. 'Tomorrow,' said Phena, 'I'll go and say goodbye to my aunt and collect a suitcase and some clothes she's giving me. But today we can do as we like.'

'I wonder where Davey's gone,' said Triffy.

'Maybe to Sidmouth to do some shopping.'

'I bet he's gone to find the blue gromwell so he can get the money from Mr Bond. Why don't we go to Weston and keep a lookout?'

Phena agreed and they set off. As they began to descend into Sheepwash Vale, Phena said abruptly, 'Look, I can see one of Pete Derryman's gang, up there by the gate.' As Triffy glanced across the vale, three more boys appeared, and then two girls. 'Pam and Sally,' said Phena grimly. 'Shall we go back?'

'No, now's our chance to get even. I'll make them run for their lives. She took out her catapult and began to look for stones. 'You go ahead and meet them.'

As the children moved down the slope, Phena noticed that Pam and Sally were carrying old-fashioned broomsticks made with twigs and tied with string. Her tormentors surrounded her and shrieked, 'Want a broomstick, you ugly witch?'

Then the twins began to poke at her with the broomsticks. 'Here then, let's see you ride away!' and Sally thrust hers at Phena.

'Go on,' said one of the boys, 'get on your broomstick. If you're a witch you should be able to fly away.'

'Yes, we want to see you fly!' shouted the twins.

At that moment a small stone hit Sally on the shoulder, followed by one that caught Pam on the arm. Soon each of the gang had been sharply stung by a stone or a stick. They stopped jeering at Phena and fell silent, looking around suspiciously. Then Triffy came up close to Pete and clawed at his face with a prickly branch of hawthorn. 'Let's get out of here!' commanded Pete, and the children all ran as though their lives depended on it.

'They won't bother you again,' said Triffy gleefully. 'I really enjoyed that!'

But Phena wasn't so happy. 'They'll tell their parents what happened, and if I was to stay in Branscombe, I'd be in trouble.'

But Triffy, in this respect rather like her father, never thought too far ahead. It was impossible to predict what would befall Phena and herself, and they could only live day by day.

★

They swam off Weston beach, and now Triffy had a serious problem. The sole of one of her trainers had fallen out as she picked it up, so how was she going to carry on in bare feet?

'You'll be all right,' said Phena. 'You can't get hurt as a ghost, can you?'

'It does hurt,' said Triffy.

'Well, let's go up to Sweetcombe Farm, and I'll say those boys hid my shoes to tease me, and ask if I can borrow some. They might even give me an old pair. I've seen lots of boots lying round their back porch.'

Triffy found it impossible to bound up the cliff as fast as Phena, and halfway she sat down to rest. When she rose to continue, she heard raised voices. At the stile she was aghast to see Davey clutching Phena's arm and shouting, 'Show me where it is, or you'll be sorry! Bond has now promised us one hundred guineas!'

'I won't!' cried Phena, struggling to get away from his grasp. As Triffy hastily clambered over the stile, uncle and niece became engaged in a furious contest near the edge of the ravine. She looked for something to throw, but could only find a few small stones. She aimed them at Davey, but they made no impression. She could only watch with mounting horror as her fragile wisp of a friend attempted to stand up to Davey's brute strength – kicking, writhing and scratching, and eventually biting him. This only goaded him to the limit, and the force of his vicious temper enabled him to heave Phena off the ground and toss her over the hedge into the deep ravine, yelling, 'The devil take you then!'

He stood panting on the edge as Phena disappeared into the dense, thorny undergrowth. Then hastily he climbed over the stile and started down the cliff. Triffy followed until he stopped at the bend. She came up behind Davey, intending to push him down the almost vertical incline. If she hadn't been a ghost she would have succeeded. As it was, he felt nothing. He stood looking for a while, and then changing his mind, he climbed back to the stile and began to walk up the field towards the woodland.

Triffy stood staring down at the ravine in a state of shock. Nothing stirred below her, and anyone passing would never have guessed that a girl was lying on the stream bed under the thick mass of growth. Her first thought was to try getting down to the bottom of the ravine, but without shoes it was too difficult. Even if Phena was still alive, Triffy couldn't carry her out. Since she was invisible, how was she to communicate the disaster to anyone in this world of 1912? Full of misery and confusion she started the long painful walk in bare feet, first to Sweetcombe Farm and then along the lane towards the plats.

On the way she had an idea. If she could find paper and pencil she could write a message and place it in front of Jack, or take it to someone else if Davey had already reached the linhay. Fortunately Jack was on his own, slumped at the table as usual, staring into space. If only she could talk to him, make him move, force him to do something for his daughter for once. How she loathed his cowed way of sitting and his vacant defeated eyes!

In Phena's chest she found a pencil and a paper bag. On it she hurriedly scrawled, 'DAVEY HAS THROWN PHENA INTO THE RAVINE AT WESTON. GET HELP.'

Jack was so deep in his own thoughts that it took him a moment to notice the message on the table. When he read it, his face turned an ashy grey colour. He read it again, but still he didn't move. Triffy shouted in fury, 'Get up, tell someone, you stupid man!' In exasperation, she snatched up the paper bag and was about to dash out of the linhay when Davey entered.

'You killed Phena!' croaked Jack.

'What are you talking about?' growled Davey.

'There was a message on the table.'

'Where is it?'

'It's gone. You threw my daughter into the ravine!'

Davey's hard eyes were frightened now as he said defensively, 'What if I did? She deserved it, the obstinate little fool! Who brought you the message?'

'No one,' sobbed Jack. 'It just appeared on the table, written on a paper bag.'

Davey seized his brother by the shoulders. 'Well, where is it, you blubbering idiot?'

'I don't know,' moaned Jack.

Davey glanced into the bedrooms and then said, 'We'll have to get away from here in double quick time before they come to find us.' Jack continued to sob loudly, saying they must rescue Phena; she might still be alive. If she was dead, he wanted to stay for the funeral. He wished he'd been a better father, he wished he'd never been born.

'Alive or dead, we'll be in trouble. So we've got to hide till we get on that boat on Monday morning.'

'We can't go and leave her!'

Davey's voice was harsh with impatience. 'D'you want to stay and be hanged? D'you want to go to the workhouse? Someone knows we've killed Phena.'

'I didn't kill Phena!' protested Jack in terror. 'It was you!'

Davey grasped him by the neck. 'Listen, you idiot, we're in this together. If you don't fancy supporting me, you'll find yourself going the same way as your daughter. Is that understood?'

'Yes, Davey,' gasped Jack.

'Right. Get the rest of our things into the trunk and let's be off. I shan't be sorry to leave this linhay. Something very odd's going on round here.'

★

Triffy had listened to this conversation in horror, still clutching the paper bag. She must find someone else to show it to. But who? It was early evening and there was no sign of life on the plats.

Then she thought of old Amos, living at the bottom of the cliff, and she hurried down as fast as she could. She found him cleaning out plant pots and placed the paper bag in front of him. He peered at it in surprise. Then he picked it up, screwed it into a ball and put it in his pocket.

Almost crying with frustration, Triffy remembered that Amos had very poor sight. She climbed back slowly and painfully to the linhay. The men had departed and she lay on her bed too exhausted to think of any further action that day. *I'm the only witness to Davey's wicked deed*, she thought, *and when the cliff farmers find Davey and Jack have gone they'll think Phena's gone with them. Her body may not be found for months, even years*. So tomorrow she must write another message and deliver it to

Dulcie. If that didn't work, she must return to the ravine herself and attempt to pull Phena's body out of the undergrowth so it could be seen from above. How stupid she had been not to do that straight away! Now she was too tired to make another journey.

She noticed Phena's wild flower book lying on the chest and put it in her rucksack. Then she burst into tears, thinking of her friend lying in the ravine. It was just possible that Phena might still be alive. However difficult the task, she must go back to Weston at once and see. But a few seconds later she fell sound asleep, unable to deal with any more problems that day.

CHAPTER 17

S he woke with a violent start from a dream in which she had been falling down a cliff. Her first thought was Phena's body. *I must go and find it.* Then immediately she knew she had returned to her old life. It was still dark, but she could see enough to realise she was in a large room with two windows. She was lying on the comfortable sofa where she had fallen asleep on first reaching the plats. Through the open windows she could hear the jazz music and the chatter of guests. What time could it be? Was it an all-night party? And how amazing that no one had yet come into the chalet.

Like a guilty thief she rose, grabbed her rucksack and dashed into the garden and out of the gate. Daybreak was not far off. A thin, glittering line of light ran along the horizon and already birds were singing. The atmosphere held nothing of the freshness of the early May mornings she had become used to. It must be July again. The air had scarcely cooled during the night, and soon the sun would rise in a clear sky and burn off the few pockets of sea mist clinging to the cliff side, now covered once more with dense woodland.

It was only when she started walking along the path that she realised she was wearing the old trainers again. She reached the humps and sat on the grass. Yesterday spring flowers had covered these humps, but today they had largely been replaced by the flowers of high summer. Far below, the calm sea was a dark blue with lakes of paler blue spread across it.

For a while, she did wonder whether her experience on the plats had just been a vivid dream, but when she opened her rucksack and took out the book on wild flowers, she knew it was no dream. Besides, there was the gold ring on her finger.

Suddenly she was overwhelmed by the thought that Phena's body would no longer be in the ravine, that Phena had died years ago and was lost to her for ever. And Phena meant more to her than anyone else, even her dad.

Triffy tried to adjust her mind to being back in her real life. Now, of course, everyone in the village would be able to see her. She had disliked the strange experience of being a ghost, but now she almost dreaded being seen, particularly in her scruffy clothes.

First she must find the cottage where Mrs Garland lived. How useful that she already knew the quickest way to Branscombe! The woods above the church looked familiar enough, yet there was something different about them. Possibly there were fewer trees, or maybe the heat wave had dried up the undergrowth. Certainly the actual path had changed, for there was a series of built-in steps down the steepest sections. When she reached the stile at the edge of the woods, she noticed that the long grassy valley bed was dry and the mud round the little footbridge was baked hard. Two wooden seats had appeared at the bottom of the churchyard next to the old kiln below the yew trees. Rows of small modern headstones stood in rows on the west side of the church, but the ancient lichen-covered tombstones and the many table tombs, were still there.

There were changes inside the church too. The new pews, looking much less shiny, had been enhanced by rows of colourful kneelers embroidered in tapestry work, many of them inscribed with the name of a king or queen. She looked up at the slender modern cross above the nave, and the wrought iron lamp holders now hanging from the roof. She sat down on one of the kneelers, assuming it was a cushion, and braced herself to walk down the village street in such a sorry state.

Her fears returned of being apprehended and taken back to the children's home before she found her grandmother. But at least it wasn't far from the church to the forge and the long pink cottage in which, with luck, Mrs Garland would still be living. Cars and holidaymakers were already moving along the road as Triffy ran down the hill, stopping short when the thatched forge came in sight. Yes, there was the pink cottage, with two tiny windows at one end. There was the bakery and the stream and the stone-faced village hall with a clock above the door. Beyond were rows of modern houses.

With a pounding heart she approached the pink cottage, and to her amazement, found it was divided into number one and number two Blacksmith Cottage. On which of the two green doors should she knock? She began to peer into the open windows in the hope of seeing someone who might be her grandmother. But, in contrast to the brilliant sunshine outside, the interiors were too dark to see anything.

Suddenly the door of number two opened, and a severe-looking woman said angrily, 'What a cheek! Haven't you been taught better manners than to go poking your head into people's houses?' Triffy stared up at the tight, unsmiling face, and was reminded clearly of the last occasion she had stood at this door. This was definitely her grandmother, and the sight was not promising. Harriet Garland still wore the iron-grey plait wound round her head, and she still had the same pinched lips and tired eyes. Her faded cotton dress hung limply over her stick-like figure, and her down at heel shoes looked rather tight over her swollen blue-veined feet. Triffy's heart sank as she realised that this woman wasn't well off, and might be quite unable to keep her.

'I'm Triffy Garland,' she stated boldly, and then continued in a rush, 'my mum's dead, and my dad's got a new girlfriend. She didn't like me, so I was put in a children's home. But now I've run away and I want to live with you.'

'And where might your father be living?' demanded Harriet.

'I don't know. He never came to see me,' said Triffy, looking pathetic. 'I've been in the children's home for two years.'

'Trust Ken,' said Harriet bitterly. 'And what makes you think I could afford to look after you? I don't like kids, and you look a right little scruff in those dreadful trainers!'

'I had to walk all the way from Sidmouth to find you.'

'How long did it take you?'

'All night, along the coast path.'

'The coast path! What a dangerous way to come. You might have fallen over the cliff. And a child shouldn't be out alone at night.'

Although Harriet spoke in a scolding tone, she was secretly thinking her granddaughter must have been very unhappy in the children's home to undertake such a long walk by night on a steep cliff path. And what dirty clothes the child was wearing. What kind of children's home could it be? At the same time she thought of all the difficulties she would face with the social services, and the responsibility of caring for a child. So she said, 'Well, you'll have to go back to Sidmouth in a while. I'm too old to look after you. What use would you be? I daresay you've learnt nothing from your parents. Can you cook?'

'No. Mum never cooked. We lived on takeaways and baked beans.'

'You haven't even brought any clothes with you. I can't afford to buy you things.'

The trauma of the last twenty-four hours had made Triffy feel very weak and quite unable to stand up to her grandmother's questioning. Tears began to trickle down her cheeks, making her look more destitute than ever. Harriet was stirred, not so much by the tears, as by the idea that this small thin, grimy child, had walked so far to reach Branscombe. Her own life had been a struggle, and she admired toughness of purpose in others.

'Well, you'd better come in and have something to eat and a good sleep before you go back.'

'If you're going to send me away, I'll go now,' retorted Triffy angrily, and she started to walk off up the hill.

'Don't be silly, child!' Harriet shouted after her. 'Come back and we'll talk about it.' Triffy returned, and Harriet led the way through the living room into the kitchen at the rear of the cottage. Triffy followed slowly, taking time to glance round at the shabby furnishings of her grandmother's front room – the worn multicoloured carpet, the gate-leg table covered with a green chenille cloth edged with white bobbles, the threadbare three-piece suite, the veneered coffee table and a three-tiered chrome cake stand. And yet again, she noticed the half-dozen frames on the wall containing samples of handmade lace similar to those in Dulcie's cottage.

'Does everyone here make lace?' she asked.

'Goodness, no, not these days. My grandmother and my mother made the lace in those frames. It's slow work, and I haven't the patience.'

After washing her hands and face, Triffy sat down at a scrubbed wooden table in the kitchen and ate two boiled eggs with toast and marmalade.

'Why did you run away? Weren't they kind to you?'

'It was okay, but I hated being bossed around all day. And they wouldn't let me go out alone.'

'The police will be looking for you by now.'

'They won't look here because they don't know I've got a gran living in Branscombe.'

'Maybe not, but I'll have to let them know you're here.'

Triffy jumped up and made for the door.

'Sit down, you stupid girl. Of course I have to let them know. You'll have caused a lot of worry.'

'What will you say?'

'That I intend to adopt you,' answered Harriet grimly.

Triffy sat down again, feeling reassured, though her grandmother hadn't smiled once. It wasn't going to be easy living with this bitter woman, but Triffy felt she was an honest person with a sense of duty. It might be preferable to the children's home, or it might not.

'It'll be a hard life with me because I haven't much money,' said Harriet. 'Children expect so much these days. I sacrificed a lot to give your father all he needed, and what did he do but throw his life away. He'll be no help in my old age, but maybe you will.'

'Do you live alone here?' asked Triffy.

'My mother, who's in her nineties, used to live with me, but she had to go into a nursing home. She can't walk and she's very frail. I doubt she'll last the year. You can come upstairs now and have a bath. Then you can put on my dressing gown while I go out and find you something to wear.'

CHAPTER 18

The room Triffy was to sleep in had been her father's as a child. There were pictures of motorbikes cut out of magazines on the white walls. On the chest of drawers, stood a model of a racing car he had put together from a kit. Apart from the narrow bed covered with a faded yellow candlewick bedspread, the room was almost entirely filled with cardboard boxes and a sewing machine. Green curtains decorated with a pattern of ships, hung at the one small window. Triffy felt quite comforted being in her father's old room. It was as though she had come home at last, in spite of her gran's unwelcoming attitude.

'I keep my upholstery materials in here,' Harriet said. 'You'll have to put up with that.'

Having a bath seemed very strange to Triffy. She lay in the tub for twenty minutes, until the water became thick with grime. Harriet had left an old, rather scratchy towel on the rail. When Triffy returned to the kitchen, Harriet said, 'I'm going down to the tourist shop on the beach, on my bike, to buy some clothes for you to be going on with until I can get to Seaton. You can peel the potatoes while I'm gone, and cut up half this cabbage.'

Before leaving, Harriet tuned into Radio Two for music to keep her granddaughter company. But Triffy had become used to silence, and the music seemed very raucous.

After life in Davey's linhay, cleaning vegetables was so much easier with water from a tap, that Triffy quite enjoyed the task. Afterwards, she explored the drawers and cupboards in the downstairs rooms. She found nothing of interest, other than an album containing photos of her father as a grinning, cheeky-looking boy. It was amazing how little he had changed. Then she went into the small garden where a row of washing was suspended over a patch of lawn. Beyond lay a vegetable garden with green beans and gooseberry bushes and a couple of ancient apple trees. So this was now to be her home. It was luxury compared to the linhay.

Harriet returned with a pair of shorts and some cheap canvas shoes. 'I've rung the police, and a social worker is coming to see me tomorrow.'

'Will I get sent away, d'you think?' asked Triffy.

'You might when she finds I'm not well off. And being over seventy won't help.'

'They ought to give you some money for taking care of me.'

'That's what I'm hoping. I'll have to buy you some school uniform for a start. And just remember, if you want to stay with me, there'll be no doing just as you please. I shall expect you to help about the house and in the garden.'

Triffy stared at her grandmother and knew she had met her match. But she didn't mind. It wouldn't be half as bad as the slavery Phena had put up with.

'D'you want to sleep now?' asked Harriet.

'No, I'm not tired any more.'

'Well, why don't you go out and look around the village and walk down to the beach? I usually spend half my day doing upholstery, so you'll have to find yourself some friends to talk to for the rest of the school holidays.'

'I don't want any friends,' said Triffy.

'Of course you must make friends. You can't be stand-offish in a village. I'll not have it said you're one of these problem children. I had enough trouble with your father causing a scandal. You must fit in or go back into care.'

There were so many holidaymakers in Branscombe that none of the village children took much notice of Triffy. Now that she had found her grandmother, her thoughts went back to Phena. She must go back to the churchyard and find out if her body had been buried there. But when she scanned the lettering on the headstones, she only found Alice Edgecombe, Phena's mother, and a Charles and Katherine Edgecombe, presumably Phena's grandparents; no sign of Phena Edgecombe. So where could she be buried?

The horrible thought came to her that perhaps since that evening in 1912, no one had discovered Phena's body. Her skeleton might still be lying in the ravine. And if a skeleton was found now, no one would know it was Phena's, and who would believe that Triffy had any knowledge of her death? How could she begin to explain her strange experience when she herself couldn't understand how she had strayed into an earlier decade and become a ghost of the future? Triffy worked out that there might be a few elderly residents in Branscombe who had been cliff farmers and who might recall the name of Edgecombe. But how could she ask without giving herself away?

★

After lunch, Triffy set forth again, having assured her gran that she would keep away from the edge of the cliffs. Equipped with shoes and a good meal inside her, Triffy was able to reach Weston Cliff in less than an hour. She noticed at once that the ravine was as she had first seen it before meeting Phena. The sides were cleared of scrub, and the stream was no longer engulfed in thick vegetation. Now there was an easy way into the ravine from the beach.

Down by the stream, which had partially dried up in the heat wave, it was very hot and claustrophobic. There was no sign of anything which might have been part of Phena. Triffy shuddered and felt faint. The thought of her friend dying down here all alone, and then not ever being found and buried was too horrible to contemplate.

It was getting late by the time Triffy climbed out of the ravine and set off for Branscombe. She was vague when Harriet asked where she had been. 'Just wandering about,' she said.

'There's a couple of sisters living down the road that you could make friends with. I know their mother very well.'

But Triffy wasn't interested. She wanted the rest of the holidays to herself, to try and find Phena. Since she herself had been a ghost, perhaps Phena might come back to the plats as a ghost from the past to explain what had happened to her body?

The following day, a social worker called and spent most of the morning asking questions and sorting out Triffy's future. To her relief, it was settled that she should live with her grandmother for a year, and then the situation would be reviewed.

The heat wave had come to an end, but the weather was still warm and fairly dry. Every afternoon for the next two weeks, Triffy spent her time on the cliffs. Triffy mentioned to her gran that she had crossed the plats on her way to Branscombe and noticed the chalets.

'Those are holiday homes,' said Harriet. 'Though goodness knows why anyone should want a chalet on that steep cliff.'

A few of the holiday chalets on the plats were still occupied, including Davey's linhay, so Triffy couldn't look for Phena there. Often she heard laughter behind the high hedges and met people who stared at her in surprise, and sometimes with suspicion. Once she ventured down to the green and white chalet where the dog had attacked her, but the place was now unoccupied and the gate padlocked. She was able to squeeze through the hedge and gorge herself on crab apples at the very table where she had pinched the sausages.

How terrified she had been that day, and how confident she felt now! It was as though after all she had been through with Phena, she had some special claim on the plats. In a few days she knew every inch of every path, every deserted chalet, every hollow and spring and tree. Just as she had learnt in Sidmouth how to slip out of sight, so she could disappear silently into the undergrowth at the slightest sound of humanity. And each day she would learn the names of a few more wild flowers, using Phena's book as a guide.

Sometimes she sat on Eli's Seat and shut her eyes and wished very hard for Phena to appear. Once, as she was walking across the humps at sunset, she thought she saw Phena on the cliff below her, walking along in her brown skirt and sun bonnet. Her heart thumping with joy, she yelled, 'Phena! Wait! I'm coming down!'

But when she came to the place where her friend had been, there was no one in sight. She burst into tears, and then had to flee as an elderly couple came down the path in her direction.

On another occasion, as she was sitting on the cliff top just above the western entry to the plats, she heard the braying of a donkey and caught sight of the familiar figure leading Topsy towards Weston. Once again she leapt up and hurried to catch up with Phena, but by the time she reached Kiln Lane, the vision had disappeared.

Several more times Triffy thought she saw Phena on the plats, always at a distance. If she was halfway down, Phena might be silhouetted at the top. If she was near the top, Phena would be seen sitting on Eli's Seat or perched on an upturned boat on the shingle. The sightings were always at dusk, amid little swirls of mist. It became a fruitless search, and each tantalising glimpse of Phena was very unsettling. Triffy became completely obsessed with the idea of contacting her lost friend.

Harriet was surprised to find how easy it was having Triffy in her house. Though the child had a mind of her own, she was no trouble. Any free time she had, after helping with the chores was spent, so she said, in pursuit of wild flowers. Each time she went out she carried in her rucksack the heavy, old-fashioned book on plants. Harriet had feared that her granddaughter might be bored and become a burden. Never had she imagined that Triffy would be so content to roam about the countryside alone. Yet there was something odd about the child which Harriet couldn't quite pin down.

At the end of August, a Mr and Mrs Dixon, near neighbours of Harriet's, told her they had seen Triffy on the plats in tears. The elderly couple had been cliff farmers in their youth and were accustomed to taking the occasional evening walk to the plats to recall old times. They had been surprised to find that Triffy had discovered the paths across the plats so quickly. Most children in the village had no idea they existed. Harriet herself had never walked along the cliff paths. When she asked her granddaughter why she went so often, Triffy replied, 'Because there's lots of wild flowers on the cliffs.' Harriet didn't pry any further, but she felt there was something unusual about Triffy's anxiety to dash off alone every day, wet or fine, to look for plants. Triffy needed something new to occupy her mind and above all, she ought to have friends of her own age.

By the time Triffy started at the village school, she had by no means given up hope of communicating with Phena again, but she found school life pleasant enough. The teachers were relaxed and sympathetic, and knew how to make the lessons stimulating. The children were friendly at first, but soon decided Triffy was rather peculiar. They giggled behind her back, but left her alone. Triffy didn't care. She wasn't bothered about meeting her classmates out of school. At four o'clock she would rush home to have a quick drink, stuff a few biscuits into her pockets and run off to the cliffs.

CHAPTER 19

September went by and the summer flowers began to fade. Soon the scent of smoke and damp leaves heralded the end of autumn. The seed heads of thistles blew around to be snatched up by the tiniest of birds, the goldcrest. The air smelt of winter, as the swifts dived and screamed across a sombre grey sky above the plats. Rain swept out of sullen clouds and dashed against the cliffs. Yet still Triffy trudged up to the plats along muddy paths, always hoping; hoping that one day she would be able to speak to Phena.

The evenings were drawing in and soon she would be unable to visit the cliffs after school. Harriet began to worry about her granddaughter. She was getting thinner and she would sit for long periods lost in thought. Once it became too dark to go out, she spent much time copying the wild flowers from Phena's book onto sheets of paper. She became quite adept at drawing. When spring came, she thought, she would go out and sketch the live flowers. She would become a botanist and achieve what Phena had wanted to do.

Harriet couldn't understand why Triffy didn't want to watch television after supper. There was something almost too quiet and well-behaved about the girl. Her own son, Ken, had been the opposite. He'd always been in trouble of some kind and she had never got on with him. It had been her everlasting disappointment. Triffy, in her way, was rather disappointing. In the evenings Harriet would have liked to chat, to play cards, to teach her how to sew. She wanted to make friends, but Triffy's mind always seemed to be elsewhere and she would give such vague answers when questioned. The only subject she appeared to be interested in, apart from flowers, was the plats. Since Harriet was born and bred in Sidmouth, and had only come to live in Branscombe when she married, she knew no details about the life of the cliff farmers.

'Why did they stop growing vegetables on the plats?' asked Triffy.

'Maybe because the first world war started,' replied Harriet. 'All the young men were called up to be soldiers, and the older men had to run the farms. After the war, cars and buses and trains became common and people could leave Branscombe to work elsewhere. Working the plats was very hard for very little pay. Then came the second world war and the plats became neglected.'

'Who built those holiday chalets?'

'The Broomhill family who have lived at Humps Farm for years. They own that stretch of coast and it was a good way of making money out of unused land.'

'I wish the holidaymakers didn't come to the plats,' said Triffy.

Harriet laughed. 'Why should it matter to you?'

'They spoil the plats. You think you're on your own in a secret woodland, and suddenly they appear, making a noise and looking at you as though they own the cliff.'

'Well, you don't have to go there. There are plenty of other quiet woodlands round Branscombe.'

'I like the plats best,' insisted Triffy.

'It's a dangerous place in the winter,' said Harriet. 'I don't want you going up there again until the spring.'

One Sunday, Harriet asked Triffy if she would like to visit her great-grandmother in the nursing home at Seaton. Triffy half wanted to go, but she desperately needed to make one more visit to the plats, so she declined. After all, what was the point of meeting a dying old lady? When her grandmother had gone, she put on her rubber boots and anorak, and made her way cautiously through the slippery mud and wet leaves and puddles, to Davey's linhay. It was satisfying to know that at this time of year she was probably the only person on the plats. Under the trees it was dark and gloomy, and had she not known it so well she might have been scared.

As she approached the linhay she realised, first with shock and then with delight, that she wasn't looking at the holiday chalet, but at Phena's home. Her heart began to beat wildly as she thought, this time, surely this time, Phena would be there and they would be able to talk. Everything would be explained.

She crept quietly to the window and peered into the hot smoky room. She recoiled at the sight of Davey and Jack sitting at the table playing cards and drinking. But they did not look up. Then Phena came out of her bedroom, wearing a long hand-knitted cardigan, and Triffy exclaimed, 'Hi, Phena!' and banged on the window pane before she could stop herself. But there was no reaction from within. The girl was oblivious of her presence. She walked to the kitchen range and began to stir something in a pot.

Then Triffy realised this was not the eleven-year-old Phena she had known, but a younger version. This girl hadn't yet met Triffy. She was a stranger. What a bitter disappointment! She went on staring at the three people she knew so well, but now it was like watching a film, she had no part in it.

It was now quite dark and she had to use her torch to find the path back to Branscombe. Suddenly a new thought struck her. Time was playing horrible tricks! In order to find out what had happened to her friend's body she would need to speak, not to the Phena she had known in Davey's linhay, but the ghost of the dead Phena. And her ghost would be more likely to haunt the ravine at Weston. That was where she must look for Phena. But the more she considered it, the more uncertain she became. Did she really want to see Phena's ghost? What would she look like? How would she speak? It was an unnerving thought. Better not to know where she was buried. She would prefer to meet the Phena she had known. And she felt sure Davey's linhay was the place where it might happen.

Harriet was angry when she arrived back at the cottage spattered with mud and looking pale and miserable. 'You've been to the plats, haven't you?'

'Yes, I was quite safe.'

'I told you not to go till the spring. I've been worried stiff, knowing you were out in the dark on that cliff. Mr Broomhill from Humps Farm warned me that out of season he had sometimes found some odd characters squatting in the chalets. It's no place for a child to be wandering about. You must promise not to go again until I've given you permission, or I won't allow you out alone.'

'Okay,' agreed Triffy, sullenly.

It was going to be agonising waiting till spring, but she must do as her grandmother told her if she was to be free to roam around on her own.

CHAPTER 20

In January, Harriet said, 'I'm going to have tea with my neighbours, the Dixons. You might like to come with me and speak to them about the plats. They used to be cliff farmers in their younger days.'

Triffy went along in excitement, planning the questions she would ask. If only they'd been alive at the time Phena died. It would be impossible to ask about the Edgecombe family herself, but she hoped the Dixons might mention them.

The Dixons had been one of the last couples to work the plats, and they chatted on for most of the afternoon about the hardships of fertilising and watering the soil, harvesting the teddies, looking after the donkeys and making the journeys to Weston and Sidmouth.

'The tomatoes did so well on that warm cliff,' said Mrs Dixon. 'Some farmers even grew grapes and made wine. Of course, in the old days before the first world war, they grew wheat and barley and oats, but later there was no need. It would have been a good, healthy life if we hadn't been so poor.'

'I had other work,' added Mr Dixon, 'so it wasn't so bad for us, but there were some who could get no employment once tractors and other farm machinery came into use.'

'Yes, we had some good times on the plats,' continued his wife. 'We were all in it together, and there was always help if someone was ill.'

'Did you ever hear of some nasty men on the plats?' asked Triffy.

The Dixons looked a little surprised. 'Not as far as I know. The ones we knew were all very decent folk,' said Mr Dixon.

'Did anyone actually live on the plats?'

'One or two over the years. But most of us just went up there each day to work.'

'Did you ever hear of anyone falling down the cliff or down the ravine at Weston?'

'No, we were all pretty good at running up and down those cliffs.'

'Do you know if anyone called Davey ever lived where that holiday chalet is now, the one called Davey's linhay?'

'When we were farming, Davey's linhay was just a derelict hut. We never knew who Davey was,' Mr Dixon told Triffy.

'Now that you mention it,' put in Mrs Dixon, 'I do recall that the site was said to be haunted and that's why the linhay was left to rot.'

'Why was it haunted?' Triffy demanded eagerly.

'I'm sorry, my dear, I don't know the story. Once you could have asked old Mr Wilkins or Mr Gush who were alive at the time, but they died recently.'

'Do you know who lives at Cotthayne Cottage?'

'The Taylors had it when I was young, but it's been sold a good few times since then.'

So Triffy drew a blank. The Edgecombes and their descendants had been forgotten.

'You seem to like exploring the plats,' said Mr Dixon. 'Now that the orchard and tillage is smothered in wild growth, it's become a good place for birds.' He reeled off the names of birds she might look out for – wood pigeons, treecreepers, nuthatches, woodpeckers and tawny owls – birds she had never heard of. 'I could lend you a book if you like.'

'Your gran says you like wild flowers,' added Mrs Dixon. 'You'll find quite a few rare ones on the cliffs, especially the blue gromwells on Weston Cliff. You'll have to wait till April to see those. You'll find some on the Hooken landslip too. A lovely blue colour they are.'

Triffy was delighted to think that the plants had spread as Phena had hoped, especially the one they had saved together on the Hooken landslip. But the mystery of Phena's death remained.

At the end of January, Triffy came across the first snowdrops, and soon after a clump of early primroses creating a pool of pale yellow in the muddy brown undergrowth. Now the spring was coming, she could resume her search for Phena. But February brought a spell of frosty weather with ice on the roads, and her grandmother said no, she must wait. However, during the half-term week it became unusually sunny and warm, and Harriet relented. After breakfast, Triffy fairly raced up the muddy path from the church, as sure-footed as ever Phena had been. The trees were still bare, but spring growth was beginning to spread over the plats. She felt a new surge of hope as she approached Davey's linhay and squeezed through the hole in the hedge. A few dried-up fuchsia flowers clung to the bushes, and the garden shed was covered with brown leaves and rotting crab apples. The curtains in the chalet windows were drawn and the birds were silent.

Triffy stood for a long period willing the chalet to be transformed into Phena's home. Perhaps if she were to go inside it might happen, but how was she to enter? She walked round to the back where several trees bent over the chalet. A skylight had been let into the sloping roof, and Triffy noticed its wood was rotten and the hinges broken. If she were to climb onto the sturdy branches of the nearest tree and lower herself onto the roof, she could probably pull the window open. Tomorrow she would come again and attempt to get in.

Unfortunately, the next day Harriet insisted on taking Triffy by bus to do some shopping in Exeter, and by the time they reached home it was after four. When her granddaughter asked if she could go out, Harriet demanded to know exactly where she was going. In her determination to visit Davey's linhay that day, Triffy lied to her grandmother for the first time. 'Susan Marsh has asked me to her house to watch a video.'

'Very well, I expect you home at half past seven.'

Putting her torch and a pair of secateurs into her rucksack and some spare clothes and her catapult, just in case, she reached the linhay in twenty minutes. It proved to be an easy job to heave open the rotting window and to climb in. She opened one of the curtains a few inches and then sat on the sofa and shut her eyes, but nothing happened. She grew impatient, feeling a great sense of anticlimax. Finally she decided to walk to Eli's Seat, where she had first entered the world of 1912.

But the stretch of path to the seat had become so overgrown since the autumn, that Triffy had to use the secateurs again and again to push her way through. By the time she reached Eli's Seat it was almost dark, and getting too cold to sit in the open, so she returned to the chalet and climbed inside again. It was half past six. She would have to go home soon or Harriet would be worried and very angry. She sat on the sofa again and lay back among the cushions as she had done that first night on the plats. If only she could stay and go to sleep here and wake to find herself in Phena's bedroom again. But it was no use, and she must hurry back to Branscombe.

It was a clear night and her eyes had become used to the dark, so she put the secateurs and torch into her rucksack and prepared to climb out through the skylight. Then she caught her breath sharply and her heart thumped as she saw a light through a gap in the living room curtain. A man with a large backpack was walking across the lawn flashing a powerful torch around the garden. Triffy ducked down on the floor, frozen with terror as the intruder approached the chalet and let the beam of his torch search out the interior, narrowly missing her body crouched under the window. She heard him trying to open the door and the front windows. Then the light moved

125

away towards the shed, and as Triffy watched, the man appeared to be lighting some kind of camping stove and pulling out a garden table. Now she could see the intruder was wearing a heavy anorak and a woolly hat. A few moments later, she could smell sausages frying.

What was she to do now? There could be no question of leaving the chalet. He would be bound to hear her. She was caught for the night, for it soon became obvious the man was not going to leave. He had placed his torch on the table and was sitting in a garden chair eating his supper. This must be one of the squatters Harriet had warned her about, thought Triffy, and she felt quite weak at the prospect of his breaking into the chalet. As it was, she must remain absolutely quiet in the dark until morning. Her grandmother would be frantic with worry, but there was nothing she could do.

Triffy lay on the sofa for the third time and began to shiver violently. In the bedroom she found a duvet and dragged it into the living room. Wrapping herself in it, she eventually fell asleep.

★

At eleven o'clock that night, Farmer Broomhill, a policeman, and a coastguard who had been searching the cliffs for several hours, had detected a light at Davey's linhay. They had apprehended a man sleeping rough in the garden shed. Then the policeman, noticing that one of the curtains in the chalet was open, shone his torch through the window, and was astonished to see Triffy asleep on the sofa.

She woke with a start to find the three men looking down at her.

'Well, young lady, we've come to take you home.'

Bewildered with sleep and shock, Triffy allowed herself to be carried off the plats, and arrived at Blacksmith's Cottage to find a distraught Harriet at the door.

'Best give her a hot drink and let her sleep till morning, before asking questions,' said the policeman. 'She was asleep in a chalet on the plats, and we've taken a man in for questioning who was dossing in the garden shed. I'll contact you in the morning.'

'I didn't stay on the plats deliberately,' said Triffy in a small voice as Harriet escorted her to bed. 'You must believe me.'

'Yes, I believe you,' replied Harriet.

But in the morning, after Harriet had had a talk with the policeman, she said to a very contrite Triffy, 'You're lucky the policeman isn't going to question you. In fact you're lucky he isn't going to arrest you for breaking and entering. I told him you'd hidden in the chalet because you were frightened of the man, but I want to know why you went to the plats at teatime, just before dark. It certainly wasn't to find wild flowers.' And though the answer Triffy gave was by no means the whole truth, it was partly the truth.

'I told you before, I just like exploring the plats. It's my secret place, and it's best in the winter when I'm the only person there.'

'Well I hope you've learnt your lesson this time. You've found it isn't such a secret place after all, even in winter. You must promise never to go again without my permission.'

'I promise.'

'You must realise,' continued Harriet, 'that the authorities might decide I'm not looking after you properly – that I'm too old to run around after you on those dangerous cliffs. Then you'd be sent back to the children's home.' Triffy was horrified at this idea. Her home was now in Branscombe with her grandmother. To be sent away was unthinkable.

CHAPTER 21

A week later, Harriet informed Triffy that her great-grandmother was very ill and might not last many more weeks. The old lady was anxious to die at home and it had been arranged that she should be brought back. 'A nurse will be coming in for half an hour each day to attend to her, but otherwise it will be up to us to make her comfortable. I won't be able to go out, so I'll have to rely on you to do the shopping and help with the cleaning,' said Harriet.

Triffy secretly hoped that her great-grandmother wouldn't last till the spring, otherwise she would have no time to herself. She was mildly curious to see the old lady, but the thought of a dying 92-year-old, didn't really appeal.

An ambulance duly arrived, and the old lady was carried upstairs wrapped in blankets on a stretcher, to the third bedroom. Harriet told Triffy that her mother was sedated to ease her pain, and she would probably sleep most of the time. For a week, Triffy did the shopping and cleaning while Harriet coped with the extra washing and ironing, and prepared light meals to tempt her mother. Triffy went up once to see the old lady, but thankfully she was asleep. She wore an old-fashioned nightcap, and all that could be seen on the pillow was a patch of wrinkled yellowish skin and two deeply sunken purplish eyelids. *How dreadful to be so old,* thought Triffy. It was impossible to imagine that this wizened creature could ever have been young.

'I don't want to grow really old,' Triffy remarked to Harriet. 'It must be very miserable to be like your mum.'

'Lots of very old people don't want to go on living,' agreed Harriet. 'But there's not much they can do about it.'

Then one afternoon at the beginning of the Easter holidays, Harriet said she would have to go to Sidmouth to visit the dentist and attend to other urgent matters. For the first time, Triffy was to be left in charge of her great-grandmother.

'I expect Mum will just sleep all afternoon as usual. I'll be home at five,' said Harriet.

'She might die while you're away!' exclaimed Triffy.

'Then you can call Mrs Brown next door.'

The possibility of seeing someone die filled Triffy with trepidation as she watched Harriet disappear in the green, yellow and white local bus.

Triffy took her wild flower book and some drawing paper into the sickroom and sat on a stool near the bed. She felt very nervous, wondering what she would say if the old lady woke up. She had always considered the white-haired, dim-eyed, over-eighties who shuffled round Sidmouth with sticks and shopping bags on wheels, to be quite different from other people. You certainly couldn't treat them as friends. There must be a special way of speaking to them, but Triffy had no idea what it was.

She was soon absorbed in her sketch, but after a while she glanced at the pillow and with a shock, saw the old lady's eyes for the first time – surprisingly large, dark eyes that still had life in them. Triffy had the impression that perhaps a real person did exist behind the corpse-like face.

'Haven't I seen you before?' came a slow quavery, but perfectly clear voice.

'I'm your great-granddaughter, Triphena,' replied Triffy.

'Triphena! You'll be Ken's child then?'

'Yes.'

The old lady fell silent for a time while Triffy continued her drawing, feeling rather self-conscious, for she was being watched intently.

'What are you doing?' came the voice again.

'Drawing a blue gromwell.'

'A gromwell! Let me see,' and a skinny, papery white hand covered with blue veins, shot out from under the sheet. 'You can draw very well. The blue gromwells will soon be blooming on Weston Cliff, but I shall never see them again,' croaked the old lady, who began to stare very hard at Triffy's right hand.

Suddenly, she said abruptly, 'Where did you get that ring?'

'I was given it.'

'By whom?'

'By a friend.'

As the old lady asked these questions, her right hand emerged from the bedclothes, and this time it was Triffy who exclaimed out loud at seeing a ring on the little finger, a silver ring with tiny fake diamonds surrounding a red stone.

'Where did you get *your* ring?'

'I was given it by my greatest friend when I was a girl,' came the reply. Then the invalid closed her eyes, leaving her great-granddaughter in a state of excited agitation.

But presently, the eyes opened once more and the old lady declared, 'You're Triffy. I knew as soon as I saw you, and then I wondered if you were still a ghost. Let me feel your hand.'

The bony, wrinkled fingers gripped Triffy's smooth young hand. 'No, you're no longer a ghost. You're real flesh and blood. Fancy you turning out to be my own flesh and blood! My own great-granddaughter!'

Questions were racing round Triffy's brain. Surely, surely, this withered, sick old lady couldn't be Phena? To think that all those weeks she had searched in vain for Phena and all the time she'd been alive in a nursing home a few miles away!

'I thought you must have died when Davey threw you into the ravine,' she said in a stunned voice.

It took a full two minutes for the old lady to gather up the strength to explain, with many pauses between sentences.

'Not quite dead. Just unconscious for a long while... Do you recall that lad, Pete Derryman, who used to torment me with his friends? Well, he was coming down the path on the other side of the ravine, to the beach where he'd left his rowing boat. Through the bushes, he caught sight of me falling down the ravine, but he didn't see who had thrown me down... He ran straight up to Sweetcombe Farm to get help, and later I woke up in hospital with broken ribs and a broken arm and leg. My arm mended well, but my leg was never the same again. I've had to walk with a crutch all my life... Pete's parents looked after me until I could walk, and then they sent me to school in Beer... At sixteen, I married Pete. Wasn't that strange? We lived with his parents for a time and then bought a cottage in Sidmouth, where Harriet was born. I came here as a widow, to live with Harriet who had married a Branscombe man.'

The old lady's last few sentences had been delivered with difficulty, and she stopped talking.

'What happened to your dad and to Davey?' asked Triffy, feeling bewildered by Phena's revelations.

'I never had news of them again. Davey probably changed his name, and I never contacted my aunt. News travelled slowly in those days. It was better to let her think I'd gone to Canada... Davey's attempt to kill me would have caused her much pain. Pete and I and his parents decided we'd let people in Beer think I'd fallen down the ravine by accident. We didn't want a scandal in the family.'

The continued effort to speak made Phena cough – a terrible, rasping sound which frightened Triffy, and yet she was desperate to hear more. The small, yellowish face on the pillow had turned an unhealthy shade of purple, and the lids closed over the dark eyes, shutting Phena's personality away. But then the lips began to move again. Triffy placed her head close to the face of her sick friend. She could just make out a few more gasping words. 'So, Triffy my dear friend, we meet again, just in time. Look after Harriet when you grow up, and remember me when you go to the plats, and to Weston Cliff to see the blue gromwells.'

Phena's head slumped to one side on the pillow, and out of her nightcap fell a long thick plait of white hair. Triffy clasped the featherweight body of her great-grandmother tightly to give it warmth and energy. All to no avail. She was holding a lifeless shell. She had always imagined it would be terrifying to be left alone with a dead body – but it wasn't. Gently, she laid Phena's head back on the pillow and kissed both sunken cheeks. Then looking down in awe at the face of her great-grandmother and her best friend, she was astonished to see a transformation. Half-shutting her eyes, she could almost imagine that the wrinkles had been ironed out and it was the young pretty, gentle face she had so recently known.

Triffy buried her head in the bedclothes and cried as she had never cried before, not even when her father said she must go to a children's home. When Harriet entered the room at five o'clock, she was most upset to see what had happened, and then a little puzzled at Triffy's prolonged distress. She felt guilty at having left her with a dying woman, and surprised at just how sensitive the child seemed to be. Harriet stroked Triffy's hair, saying, 'Don't cry any more. Your great-gran was ready to go. She'll no longer be in pain. She'll be at peace.'

CHAPTER 22

G radually Harriet and her granddaughter became friends, and by the time school started again, Triffy had cheered up considerably. She no longer had to bear the anxiety of not knowing what had happened to Phena. She marvelled again and again over the fact that they were related, and she plied Harriet with questions. To her disappointment, Harriet could tell her very little about her mother's early years. She only knew that Phena's mother, Alice, had died young and that her father had emigrated to Canada. She had no idea that Phena had lived on the plats, or how she had become crippled.

'She suffered an accident as a child. That's all I know,' said Harriet. 'Mother never spoke about her youth, and I never thought to ask. She was a very secret person, and had no close friends as far as I know.'

It was typical of Phena, thought Triffy, *not to accuse her uncle or to implicate her father in a scandal. I'm the only person in Branscombe who knows what happened.*

Now that Triffy was happy at home, she began to make friends at school. By Easter she was doing well at her lessons, and the village children stopped regarding her as a stand-offish oddity. She was still the headstrong independent girl she had always been, and she and Harriet, who were not dissimilar, had a few confrontations, but in between they got on very well. Triffy made Harriet feel younger and less bitter, and Harriet gave Triffy a secure home from which to face the world. Life

had become interesting for the first time, and she never used
the phrase *dead boring* again.

★

On Easter Monday, Harriet and Triffy were just finishing
lunch when they heard a motorbike roaring down the hill and
stopping outside the village hall. Harriet looked out of the
window at a man taking off his helmet and exclaimed,
'Goodness, Triffy, it's your father!' This time Harriet let him
in, saying, 'Well now, Ken, what a surprise!'

He placed on the table a large chocolate egg wrapped in
gold foil, saying, 'There you are, Triff!' just as though there
had been no break in their relationship.

And she replied, 'Thanks, Dad.'

'So what are you doing these days?' went on Harriet.

'I'm living in Exeter now – got a steady job in a garage
mending motorbikes. You can come home and live with me,
Triff. I'm on my own at the moment.'

Triffy stared at his handsome, still boyish face and replied,
'This is my home, Dad. Gran has adopted me. I don't need to
live with you.'

Ken looked disconcerted, almost sad, but then he grinned
and said cheerfully, 'Okay, just as you like. Stay and keep your
gran company.' He placed a twenty pound note on the table
beside the egg. 'That's for a start, Mum. I'll send you more
when I can.'

Harriet smiled. 'Don't worry. We can manage. D'you want
something to eat?'

'No, don't bother, I'll be on my way.'

They heard the motorbike roaring up the hill, and that was
that. *I may never see Dad again,* thought Triffy. But it didn't
really trouble her.

★

Every weekend, whatever the weather and with Harriet's
permission, Triffy would spend an hour or two on the cliffs,

watching the change of season and learning more and more about the wild plants growing there. That first spring after Phena's death, she saw the gromwells, intense and glittering in all their glory, spread over the face of Weston Cliff and along the Hooken landslip – reddish-purple to begin with, then turning to their eye-catching vivid blue. Halfway down at the hairpin bend, she discovered a faint trace of the path Phena had taken her along to see the gromwells. Over the years, the gorse and thorn and bramble had formed an impenetrable thicket below the ledge, completely hiding the hollow where the flowers had appeared so mysteriously. Triffy liked to think that she and Phena were the only people who had ever laid eyes on the first blue gromwell to grow on Weston Cliff.

Harriet had told her that on no account was she to trespass onto the private plots on the cliff. 'Mr Broomhill will be on the lookout, so stick to the paths.' Triffy kept away from the chalets, but she learnt to move as quietly and swiftly as an animal through the undergrowth. She discovered that there is never an instant in nature where nothing is happening, that woods hide so many secrets. She acquired the patience to lie still for long periods, and though Mr Broomhill regularly patrolled his land, never once did he hear or catch sight of Triffy. As for the chalet owners, they would have been very surprised to know how often they were observed.

In her solitary wanderings, Triffy could not help looking out for Phena. Sometimes when she emerged from the woods, she imagined for an instant that she saw her friend sitting on Eli's Seat. And once when she approached Davey's linhay in winter when it was deserted, she was sure she heard the braying of a donkey. But it was only her fancy. Phena was dead, and would never come again.

★

A year later, Triffy went with Harriet to an exhibition in a barn about the history of the plats. The whitewashed walls were covered with old newspaper cuttings, photographs, maps and descriptions of the hardships as well as the happy times experienced by the cliff farmers. Triffy discovered that cliff farmers were working a few plats as early as 1763, when the rent for each one was a shilling or two shillings a year.

'A shilling is equivalent to 5p,' said Harriet.

'That's not much,' said Triffy, recalling how Phena complained about the exorbitant rents.

'No, but at that time people in Branscombe only earned a few shillings a week.'

Triffy peered at the photographs with great interest, especially the pictures of the donkeys, though some of them were taken during the years between the wars. Then she came across a large, very faded, rather blurred picture of a girl in an old-fashioned goffered bonnet with long flaps covering her ears and hanging down to her shoulders. Underneath was a notice, saying, 'We would be glad to know if anyone in the village recognises the girl in this photograph taken before the first world war.'

The more she stared at it, the more certain Triffy became that it was a photograph of Phena. She could just make out the same large dark eyes, the same elongated face, the same thick plait hanging beneath the bonnet. There was Phena's sweet half smile. The girl seemed to be wearing a wide belt, though it was difficult to see it clearly.

But no, thought Triffy. *No, it's not a belt, it's my hands round her waist. It's the photo Dulcie took of us in her garden!*

'Look! That's a picture of my great-grandmother,' Triffy announced excitedly before she could stop herself.

'Don't be silly, how could you possibly tell?' said Harriet. 'I don't recognise it.'

'I just know it is!' insisted Triffy.

Later at home, Triffy asked Harriet if it would be possible to make a copy of the photo.

'I suppose it would.'

Triffy didn't press the point, and thought Harriet would do nothing about it. But to her great delight, on her birthday she was presented with a copy of the picture of Phena in an oval frame.

'Well, I'm glad you're so pleased,' said Harriet. 'You are a strange girl. For the life of me I can't imagine why you think it's a picture of my mother.'

'You didn't know her as a child,' came the quick reply.

'Nor did you!' retorted Harriet, laughing.

Triffy smiled, but said no more. She would keep Phena's secrets for ever.